Ambush at the Blue Licks

Charles E. Hayes

ISBN:-10 1499211414
ISBN-13: 978-1499211412

DEDICATION

To the pioneers who settled and fought for Kentucky.

SPECIAL THANKS

TO MAYSVILLE KENTUCKY ARTIST
STEVE WHITE
FOR ALLOWING ME TO USE HIS ORIGINAL ART ON
THE COVER OF THIS BOOK

TO **GRAPHICENTERPRISES.NET**
JIM AND KATHY CUMMINGS
PICTURES USED WITH THE TEXT WERE ORIGINAL
COLOR PRINTS TAKEN BY JIM CUMMING

CONTENTS

	Acknowledgements	i
	Prologue	3
1	Rumors of War	5
2	Decision Made	10
3	Leaving	18
4	Lige	23
5	Indentured Servants	30
6	Indian War	35
7	Legend and Fact	40
8	Wolf Head Tavern	38
9	Martin's Station	53
10	Cumberland Gap	59
11	McNitts Defeat	64
12	Redskins and Redcoats	72
13	Bryant's Station	79
14	Attack at Bryant's Station	90
15	Starting The Chase	112
16	The Blue Licks	120
17	Ambush At Blue Licks	127
	Epilogue	141

ACKNOWLEDGMENTS

The wonderful staffs at Martin's Station, Cumberland Gap National Park, Boonesborough State Park, Fort Harrod State Park and The Battle of Blue Licks State Resort Park, Jim and Kathy Cummings of the reenactment site, graphicenterprises.net for access to their material and the use of photos taken by Jim Cummings. I must always acknowledge the written work of Neal. O. Hammon, Dr. Thomas D. Clark, Dale Payne, Ralph Marcum, John Curry, Bennett Henderson Young and numerous others whose works I have read. The Boone Society and friends groups of the above mentioned parts. The influence of Bill York and other member of the Corps of Kentucky Longrifles and the artists, Steve White of Maysville, Kentucky and David Wright of Gallatin Tennessee.

An older frontier rifleman, one who may have survived a lot of Indian trouble.
Photograph taken by Jim Cummings graphicenterprises.net

Prologue

An Old Man Remembers

You ask me if I remember Blue Licks. I take it you mean the ambush at Blue Licks. Hell yes, I remember the ambush at Blue Licks. I was there and I remember it like it happened no more than thirty-three years ago. I was there.

I was there and that's why I've got no use for the British till this day. No use for England. No use for the British. They are a bunch of arrogant, sorry worthless asses. We whipped them and got our freedom from their damn king... Andy Jackson and me just whipped them again at N 'Orleans and by God, we can whip them again.

You do understand that our war for independence had already been won. In October 1781, General Washington whipped Cornwallis and his whole army at Yorktown, Virginia. Forced the high and mighty fancy-britches British to surrender. Cornwallis was such a low breed of man that he didn't come out himself. He sent a flunky to surrender. And that flunky tried to surrender to the French general instead of to General Washington. You can bet they set him straight in a hurry.

The true fact is the war was over except for signing a few papers. There was no reason for the bloody, scalp-buying, British to hire Indians to attack us again. The only reason I've been able to come up with is the damn British wanted to take everything west of the mountains for themselves. Then they weren't man enough to do it themselves. They had to pay a passel of hell bound savages to fight for them.

Now, thirty-three years later, I got no use for the British and I got no use for the Indians. That's just the way it is. Now Ulysses Patton, the school teacher, told me the other day that I shouldn't hate the Indians because they were just trying to keep their homes in Kentucky. Now Useless, I mean Ulysses, don't know what he is talking about.

There were no Indian settlements or towns in Kentucky when Harrod and Boone brought settlers into Kentucky. All the Indians lived south of Kentucky or north of the Ohio River. The reason Kentucky settlements were attacked so much is that the British were paying for scalps and were paying for captives. Every Indian raid on Kentucky settlements was done because the British paid the hellish savages to attack.

Noble savages Hell!! If it was up to me, we'd wipe them all out and be done with it. As far as I'm concerned we should destroy every Indian village and all of England. They're both sorry outfits and I'm glad Andy Jackson and me beat the hell out of them both.

Don't bother to argue with me. If you'd seen the bodies of babies who had their brains knocked out against a tree while their mothers screamed and watched, you'd know what I'm talking about. Damn them all.

Pour me some from that jug and I'll tell you about how it was.

1

RUMORS OF WAR

The fighting in the south, Georgia North and South Carolina, caused a lot of people in those states to pack up and immigrate to Kentucky. I know there had been fighting going on since April of 1775, when the cowardly, bloody British marched against the people of Massachusetts but were chased back to Boston with their tails between their legs. The British tried to take Charleston, South Carolina in June 1776 but got turned back. In 1778, the British managed to take Savannah down in Georgia but all in all, most of the armies and fighting were in the north. Of, there had been some scattered fighting but folks were mostly content to be peaceful. At least in the Yadkin Valley where we were.

Just like everywhere else in the colonies, I mean United States, some of the folks favored the patriot cause but a passel of them favored the British side. A whole bunch of them just wanted to be left alone. What they had in common was no desire to fight their neighbors or to be burned out by them. One of the results of the worthless British army in the Carolina's was the increased immigration to Kentucky. That's how my folks come to leave North Carolina and be in Bryant's Station, Kentucky in 1782.

My pa and ma came to the colony of North Carolina as indentured servants from Ulster, Ireland in 1748. They were lucky and got indentured together but both had to agree to work an extra year in order to stay together.   They both worked hard and helped the family holding their indenture out of a few bad spots during the eight years they were indentured.   Not all indentured servants were as lucky as my pa and ma.

My folks left their indenture to go to a small farm with a fifteen by eighteen foot log cabin with a loft at each end. There was a shed big enough for stock and a well was already dug. I wondered at that because I didn't know of any other indentured servants that left their indenture service and stepped into such a good situation. Pa never volunteered any information and I didn't ask.

We left North Carolina in June 1780. Charles Town, South Carolina had just fallen to the British and some of the folks that were partial to King George and the British decided it was time take advantage of the British victory. They banded up in packs and commenced to steal from their neighbors who favored freedom from England.

Not all of the Tories felt this way.   Our neighbor in the Yadkin Valley, Amos Patton, had Tory leanings but had no desire to fight or steal from his neighbors. Our families had always helped each other and I don't reckon had ever hit a lick at each other, except for me and Ben.

Me and Ben was both fourteen years old and we had wrestled and raced and fit and hunted together since we were six years old. Maybe even before that but if we did I don't remember. I still remember Amos and Ben coming to our farm after we learned of the fall of Charles Town.

Pa sent me to fetch a bucket of fresh, cool water when we saw them coming. We knew they would be hot and thirsty from their walk. They each drank two gourd dippers of the fresh, cool water before we started to talk.

It was already early evening when they arrived. Amos and Ben and Pa and me sat on stools and talked as we watched the sun move toward the west and over the mountains.

"John," Amos said, "we are leaving before the fighting gets here."

"What fighting?" Pa took a long draw on his pipe and continued, "I thought maybe the fighting might be all over."

"No, it aint, I've done been asked to join a group and start punishing folks that stand against the king. They want to run off or kill patriots and take their property."

"Well," Pa puffed his pipe a moment, "I hope you don't do that."

"I aint aiming to, but plenty will. Then the folks against the king will get together and fight against those favoring the king."

"Probably."

"I don't think I'm a coward and I don't think you are either, but I don't think either of us want to fight folks that were once our neighbors and friends."

"I think not. I'd rather not, but I'll fight if attacked."

"I thought that way too, but once the fighting starts and folks take sides, where'll it stop. I don't want you shooting at me or me shooting at you."

"Where you aiming to go?"

"We're leaving in three days for the Kentucky settlements. I got the idee from listening that there aint much time before trouble stops."

"I wish you luck."

"I was hoping you would go with me, the Harris and Turner families are going."

I knew this was something different. The Harris family were Tories and the Turner family was dead set against the King. I looked

7

over at Ben and he grinned at me. I could tell that he was ready to go to Kentucky. We had both talked about it often enough.

Just hearing the word "Kentucky" spoken caused us to get a little excited. Kentucky was fresh, it was new and it was waiting there for us. The woods were not strange or fearsome to us. We had both been born on the Carolina frontier to free, hard-working parents. We each had two older brothers. I had two sisters and Ben had a younger sister named Lucy.

Pa stared at the sun which was throwing the mountain's shadows back at us. "I'll think on it. It's awful short notice though."

"I got the feeling that we aint got a lot of time to decide. I was told I was either with them or against them and I don't want to be pushed into this type of mess."

"I don't blame you."

"It is not the fighting. It's that my womenfolk could wind up in the middle of it."

Pa removed his pipe from his mouth. "That's a good point. I hadn't thought they would war on women."

"I aint sure what they might do." Amos hesitated then said, "John, you know my oldest son and your girl been seeing each other."

"Yes, I'm considering that too, and Amos."

"John."

"Would you feel comfortable giving me the name of the man that wants to drive out the patriots?"

"It's Jason Smith."
Pa puffed his pipe and nodded, "Thanks."

Pa did not think much of Jason Smith. It wasn't what pa said about him that told me this, it was that he never mentioned him.

2

DECISION MADE

I don't know how Pa's considering would have come out if it had been left to him alone. Pa was a quandary kind of a man. On the one hand he was peaceful and slow to anger. On the other hand, he didn't have a lot of backing up in him. Thinking back, I don't know that I had ever seen him angry. I had seen him stern and resolute. I had seen him state his opinion and argue it but I had never seen him get all flushed and red and loud like I had seen some men. Thinking back, none of the men I had seen get all angry and disturbed got that way when they had different opinions from pa. I considered him a thinking man who avoided any ruckus.

Pa was thinking. He leaned back and smoked his pipe, saying nothing to nobody. He just stayed out in the evening air and watched the mountain's shadow grow. I think he was just considering, like he told Amos he was going to do. Ma went out to talk with him. I'm not sure what was said, but he checked the three rifles and the fowling piece when they came back in the cabin.

He drew the charge from each barrel, ran a cleaning tow down each one and reloaded with fresh powder. Then he took each flint from the cock and tested for sharpness. Just to be sure, he tapped them with a brass knapping hammer and tightened them inside the cock. Then he called me and my brothers.

"Moses, Samuel, Aaron, I want you three to divide up the night. One of you needs to be hid outside where you can see the front of the cabin all the time. Aaron, you're the youngest, you go first."

"Yes pa."

I picked up the fowler, pulled the charge again and double loaded it. I grabbed its pouch with powder horn attached and went outside. As soon as I stepped outside the cabin, my dog, Bear, came beside me. Staying next to the cabin and in the shadows, I circled the cabin three times, increasing my distance from the cabin each time. I finally stopped in some bushes about seventy yards from the cabin's door. I settled down to watch. I think I jumped every time the breeze moved a blade of grass, I jumped. Despite my best intentions, after about two hours I started to doze off.

I came wide awake when I heard the low rumble of a growl start in Bear's throat. I heard several men on horseback approaching my position. I put my hand on the back of Bear's neck to quiet him and let him know I was awake. The horses were reined to a stop. I heard people dismounting and the sounds of horses being hobbled and tied to a rope strung between two saplings. I could hear men moving close to me. I was awake, but I didn't move anything but my eyes. I could hear two people step into the dark clump of bushes with me. I could hear horses and the rest of the men close by. Someone was giving instructions in a loud whisper.

"You three go to the right front corner. Sam, you and your brothers take the left front corner. Lemuel, Joe and Josh, hold on to all the horses and guard our backs. The rest of you go to the back of the cabin."

I recognized the voice of the man giving orders. It was Jason Smith.

"Move quiet now. I'll give you time to set up and then I'll holler up the cabin."

I mean to tell you that I was some scared right then. There were at least twelve men out there and it didn't take a smart man to figure they weren't up to anything good. Everyone moved to their position. The men left with the horses tied them all to a rope that was tied tight between two strong saplings. One of them leaned his Brown Bess against a limb and sat down. From a large sack he produced a jug that he uncorked. I could hear the gurgle as he took several gulps of the whiskey.

"What the Hell?" The remaining two men heard the sound of whiskey being drunk as clearly as I heard it. They left the horses and went to where their comrade was sitting with a jug of whiskey in his lap.

"You know damn well Jase don't want us drinking."

"Then don't drink."

"Well, I'll have some," the third man interjected, "you don't have to drink if you don't want any."

Both men leaned their rifles beside the Brown Bess and took several swallows. I kept still and waited. They each had a second round and I shifted quietly to put myself in reaching distance of their firearms. No one was paying attention to me, the horses or the rifles. The three of them stood with the jug. They were facing away from me.

Someone, it sounded like Jason Smith, stopped about twenty yards in front of the cabin, beside the well, hollered out, "Halloo the cabin, halloooo the cabin."

That was when I made my move. I stepped between the three men and their weapons and hollered as loud as I could. "Yeeeeeeeeeeeaaaah!"

Now I was fourteen years old and I was scared. That holler didn't come out near as loud as it was supposed to come out. But it sure startled those three.

The three were all humped up together sharing the jug. When I squeaked, I mean hollered, they dropped the whiskey jug, and moved toward their horses and their weapons. I emptied the double charged fowler at them. I didn't aim to shoot it just then but it had a hair trigger and I was some excited and just to tell the truth, maybe a little more scared than I would have owned up to right then. Yes, I was scared. It wasn't aimed, just pointed at the three of the crowded together with the jug. The buckshot didn't have far to go but it spread a lot quicker than I would have thought. One of the buckshot hit the jug and busted it. Two of the men went down and one lit out in a hobbling run. One of the men on the ground seemed to be hit bad and the other was trying to crawl away. I clubbed him with the stock of the fowler. He went down. I pulled my knife and cut a big chunk off of his breeches.

I picked up the Brown Bess and dropped a double load of buckshot on top of the load already in it. I rammed the chunk of the man's breeches I had cut off on top to hold it in place. I pointed the Brown Bess at the shadows of three men running back to the horses from the cabin and pulled the trigger.

Judging by the roar and the kick, the brown Bess had been double charged before I had doctored the load. One of the running men went down and it was evident that two other men had caught some of the charge. I began reloading the fowler and the Brown Bess, double charging each one.

"Hiiiiii-yaaaaa," I hollered, "get at 'em boys."

The sound of a rifle shot inside the cabin sounded as loud as eternity. The shot was followed by a scream from outside the cabin. A second shot from the cabin brought another yell from outside the cabin. I saw a movement in the shadows and fired one of the rifles that had been left, then real quick fired the heavy load from the Brown Bess.

13

The shots in the dark and the squalls from the wounded were having their effect on the attackers. I reloaded in the dark, keeping the already loaded fowler close. I reloaded the Brown Bess first because it was easier to load. Then I loaded the rifle. All the while, Bear was crouched beside me. Low growls were coming from deep inside him. I heard, but didn't see, someone running toward the horses. I gave Bear a push.

"Get 'im Bear!"

Bear got him. The man screamed. There was a shot but the man kept screaming. I expected that his friends would come to help him and prepared to continue the fight when they got there. Instead, I heard Jason Smith bellow, "It's an ambush! We're surrounded! Every man for himself!"

I rescued the man Bear had down and drug him back to the bushes. I took each of the wounded men's braces and used them to tie their hands behind their backs. It was too dark to look at their wounds and I wasn't about to strike a light.

I got my breathing and excitement under control. I was surprised to find that I was shaking. I slumped back against a tree trunk and slid down it. Bear sat beside me, fully alert. After a bit, I heard a low whistle. I looked at Bear. He was alert but unconcerned about the whistle. I answered the whistle. In a few minutes, my Brother Moses came up and sat down beside me.

"God-a-mighty, little brother, you've been busy. There's one dead man out there and these three are pretty far gone."

"Anybody else hurt."

"One dead outside the cabin and one that will be soon."

"Any of us hurt?"

"None of us hurt."

"Tell pa I'd just as soon stay out here as in the cabin."

I could tell Moses wanted to argue but I guess it was a hard job to argue against what I had done. I didn't mention that I had dozed off or that Bear had really saved me. Any argument or further discussion was cut off by a throat rumbling growl from bear. Bear was crouched facing the tied and hobbled horses. His growl continued and the hair on his back was standing straight up.

Moses checked his priming and put his rifle on half cock. "Cover me," he said, and moved forward. I couldn't cover him if I couldn't see him so I followed behind him and a little to his right. I felt rather than saw movement among the horses.

"Git 'im Bear."

Bear took off like he'd been shot out of a double charged musket. In seconds, he was inside the picket line with his teeth in somebody. I could hear panting and the sound of someone running away. I fired the double charged Brown Bess at the sounds of the fleeing person and heard someone stumbling and then fall.

Moses had reached Bear and the man he was chewing on. They were easy to find because Bear's growls were much louder and the man was screaming. I went toward the sounds. I decided that I wasn't going to expose myself going to check on the man I had shot.

"Aaron, hold your dog."

"Bear."

Bear continued to growl but he came to me. Moses went over to get a better look at the man who had been Bear's chew toy.

"Aaron, its Sam Jones, by God."

"Can't be." I went over to see for myself. Sam Jones and his family sat on the bench in front of us every Sunday. I didn't want to believe it was him. It was.

Sam was bleeding from buckshot and dog bite. He was scared and crying. I was scared and mad as fire.

"Sam, what do you think you've been doing?"

"Just fighting rebels for the king, you had no right to rebellion against the king."

"You have no right to attack your neighbors."

I jumped a little and Moses did too. Pa had come up behind us so quietly that I didn't know he was there. I was surprised to see that Pa wasn't carrying a rifle. All he had was a tomahawk and a butcher knife. I noticed that both appeared bloody.

Pa was watching Bear. Bear was sitting and watching Sam. He had stopped paying attention to the area around us. Pa squatted by Sam and pulled him till their faces were only inches apart.

"Sam," Pa asked, "how many of you attacked us?"

Sam hesitated, started to lie, stared at pa and answered, "Sixteen. "

Pa got up and walked over to where the horses were tied. "There's only fifteen horses here."

Sam spoke in a hurry this time, "Joe and Josh rode double. One was going to ride your horse when we left."

"Neither one of them is going to ride anywhere again that leaves three left out there somewhere."

Moses and I just stared at each other. Neither of us had the count that high. Even with spreading buckshot from the fowler and the Brown Bess, I couldn't figure out how so many were taken down. Then I looked at the bloody tomahawk and butcher knife pa was holding. It occurred to me that the tomahawk and butcher knife didn't make as much noise as a rifle.

3

Leaving

We stayed outside after Pa returned to the cabin to tell ma, Samuel and my sisters, Sara and Susan what was going on. After pa returned to us, he put us in places where we could watch the cabin, the shed and the horses the raiders left behind. As soon as it was light enough to see, he had me take Bear and check around the farm.

"Aaron, pay attention to Bear. If Bear thinks there's something out there, then there probably is, so be careful."

I started at the cabin. What I saw there made me feel a little queasy. There were eight dead men scattered around the cabin. Six had been killed by knife or tomahawk. This was more than the two down and one killed Moses had told me. I made three more circles, each one about a hundred yards further out. I found two men, one who had died from his wounds and the other was dying as fast as he could.

On my last circle, Bear growled. I slipped into some lilac bushes where I could see without being seen. I was between whoever was coming and pa. Soon I recognized Amos and Ben riding toward the cabin. I stepped out where they could see me and waved. Ben waved back.

"Aaron," Been called, "I'm glad to see you're okay."

"Me too."

They pulled up and stopped in the shade. Amos spoke first.

"Where's your pa."

I pointed toward the cabin. Bear and I walked beside the horses. Pretty soon, we could see the man that Bear had brought down. He had bled to death from gunshot wounds and Bears kind attentions. Pa had opined that it wasn't safe risk going out to check on him.

Amos and Ben both turned a little pale at the sight but kept riding. When we got to where I'd left pa and Moses, the rest of the bodies had been drug to a dry ditch nearby. Sam Jones and three others who had survived the night were tied up out in the open. When they recognized us, pa and Moses stepped out of the brush where we could see them.

"Howdy Amos, Ben."

"John, I'm glad to see you and yours are well."

"We were lucky."

"They weren't"

"Jason Smith came by my cabin early this morning. He said you had about fifty rebels with you and you were killing all those loyal to the king."

"We aint left the farm since you left last evening."

"I see, they attacked you?"

"They tried to, didn't have much luck though."

"I'm glad you all are okay."
"Me too, when are we going to Kentucky?"

Amos was silent, apparently stunned by the question. "John, do you mean it?"

"Yeah. I don't like killing my neighbors and I don't want to be like the ones we killed last night. We leave as soon as you're ready.

"I was going to trade for some more horses."

Pa gestured toward the picket line. "We've got plenty of horses."

Amos nodded. "You mean just take up and leave today?"

"I don't feel like staying and killing any more of my neighbors."

"John, I've got to go tell Maggie that we need to leave earlier than we planned. I'll load everything up and be back by this evening."

"Amos, could you sent one of your boys for Lige Black?"

"Okay."

"Tell him I'll need him before dark and tell him to come ready to travel."

Amos nodded, "Go find him Ben."

Lige Black was a woods runner a little older than pa. I kind of wondered what pa wanted with Lige. He was a hide hunter and a market hunter who spent most of his time gone.

Pa nodded. "Amos, we got three bad wounded men here. Get word to their kin that they can come here and tend to them. Tell the dead's kin that they got burying to do. If they don't come for the bodies, I'll just push a little dirt over the whole crowd."

Pa turned to us. "Samuel and Aaron, take everything metal off of the wood. Plows, shovels, hoes, extra axes …. everything. There'll be wood where we're going but metal may be scarce."

Pa paused a moment, then continued, "Moses, start building packs that won't wear out the horses."

Pa turned to Sam Jones. "Sam, I'm surprised to see you involved in this. What in the world made you do such a thing?"

Sam looked miserable and ashamed, and not just from his wounds either. He tried to look pa in the face but found out he couldn't do it. He shook his head. "Jason Smith told us you were getting together a bunch of rebels to drive us off our farms. He said if we didn't get you first, you would get us all."

Pa shook his head. "I'm leaving. Amos is leaving. Ten men are dead and three of you are bad hurt. It looks like Jason Smith is the winner because he can move in on every farm that don't have a man to protect it. How long do you think he'll let you all live?"

Sam was stunned, he hadn't thought of that possibility. Ma and the girls came out with water and bandages. I noticed that despite all her tenderness, ma stayed between the wounded and the guns.

It was late afternoon before Amos came back with his family. He had everything loaded on a wagon. Several families were with him. The families of the three wounded and a committee to pick up the dead and take them back to their families for burial.

I was feeling a little sorry for the families of the slain and wounded. Pa, however, didn't bat an eye. He spoke harsher to the families than I had ever heard him speak.

"All these killed and wounded men came to do harm to my family and me. I got no pity for any of them. If you want to blame someone, blame the man who led them and then run off. Blame Jason Smith. He will try to move in on any farm that hasn't got a man to protect it."

Pa looked directly at each person, then said, "If I find anybody following me ---- I'll kill them. All the horses that were brought here to harm my family are mine now. All the guns brought here to harm my family are mine now."

Nobody argued. The guns, powder and lead balls had already been gathered up and packed away. Pa said we would need all of it before we were through. As soon as the dead had been hauled away and the wounded loaded onto a second wagon, everyone left.

Pa waited until the procession was out of sight. He motioned to me. When I got to him he said softly, "Aaron, take Bear and scout around. Stay hid as much as you can. Trust Bear."

I nodded and started. A low whistle from pa stopped me. Pa looked a little put out so I stepped back to him. Pa pointed to the weapons and said, "The Brown Bess is loaded with buck and ball. Take it with you and remember it don't have a lot of distance."

"Okay." I felt foolish to have started out unarmed. I was going to have to change a lot of habits, it seemed. A buck and ball load was a seventy-five caliber round ball and eight thirty-two caliber balls on top of a hundred grain load of powder.

I hadn't gone 200 hundred yards before Bear growled. I took cover and waited.

"Hey boy!!"

The voice was so close that it startled me. I thought I recognized the voice though.

"Lige?"

"It's me and it's all clear. Let's go see John."

4

Lige

Lige Black was a wood rat from scratch. I guess his proper name was Elijah, but I have never heard him called anything but Lige. He spent a lot of time in the woods west of the mountains, even as far north as Kentucky, some said. Two or three times a year, he would bring in a load of hides to sell, mostly deer hides. He didn't talk much but he always stopped by to talk to pa. I don't remember him ever accepting an invitation to come into our cabin or that he ever took a meal with us, but he always stopped by.

Pa said Lige didn't stay out as long as some others, commonly known as longhunters, because he didn't want all of his efforts to wind up in Indian hands. Lige claimed that the Indians would keep an eye on white hunters, wait until they had a good haul and rob them. Lige opined that they never killed the white hunter because they wanted him to return and hunt again. He claimed this had happened to several of the local longhunters, including Daniel Boone.

The longhunter generally came out of southern Virginia and western North Carolina. Most of these longhunters were land owners who viewed the long hunt as a business. Many of the long hunts started from the Clinch, Holston, and Yadkin valley regions. These hunters went to where there were only game or Indian paths. They learned the lay of the land in what is now Kentucky and Tennessee. Some of these longhunters like Patton, Dysart, Brooks and Knox already had some money but some had to borrow money to pay for their hunt.

When the first settlers arrived to new land that had never been touched by a plow, the longhunters and already been there and were long gone. Not only were the longhunters gone, they were by that time hunting in even more enchanting surroundings such as the Cumberland River Valley and the Ohio River. Some were as far west as the Mississippi. Some had traveled to western Kentucky and Tennessee and a few had hunted in points south and north.

The longhunters named most of the rivers and streams, gaps, salt licks, mountains and valleys long before settlers ever reached them. These longhunters were a brave and adventurous bunch. They risked hard, freezing winters in crude shelters, death from sickness, copperhead bites, accidents, hunting accidents and of course the savage Indians.

The Indians especially hated the longhunters. They looked at them as robbers. Lige always claimed that the Indians would watch a hunter and just when the hunter was ready to leave with his hides, would rob him. Lige said the reason for his shorter hunts was to keep from supplying the Indians with furs. Just why was this particular group of men given to hunting, instead of tilling the earth?

Longhunters wanted adventure. They enjoyed the companion-ship and solitude of the hunt and the wilderness. These were men like Elisha Wallen, William Carr, Isaac Bledsoe, and Daniel Boone enjoyed the hunt. At the very least, they enjoyed the hunt more than farming.

The longhunter was also a business man looking for profit. If a longhunter wasn't robbed, he could profit over a thousand dollars from a single hunting season. This thousand dollars was a sight more than he could have earned staying in the settlements.

The longhunter could foretell the weather by the way the sky looked. He could tell if the weather would be sunny of rainy. He could guide his way by using the north-star. He knew the habits of game animals and which foods were safe to eat. He knew which plants had a medical usefulness and which ones to stay away from. He could make minor repairs to his equipment and knew many habits of the Indians

Most but not all longhunters hunted from October until March or April. They hunted for both pelts and hides but deer hides was what they wanted most. A deer hide usually sold for a dollar and people began referring to a dollar as a buck.

Longhunters generally hunted in parties of two to four men. They kept hunting parties small to keep from being located by savage Indians and to keep from scaring the game off. The smart longunters knew that they would be fools to trust the savage Indians.

I heard one tale about longhunters hunting in the Powell Valley. According to the feller telling the tale, twelve miles south of Martin's Station was very rich piece of land that was called Rob Camp. There stands the remains of an old hunting camp. In 1770, three fully equipped man and six horses built a camp there. They hunted during the fall, winter and deep into the spring of the year. Now these longhunters tried to get along with the Indians while they hunted for hides and pelts. The Indians visited their camp pretty regular and bragged on what good hunters they were and all.

The longhunters allowed as they had lifelong friends in these worthless lying savages, which kind of tells me they were not the sharpest axes at the woodpile. You would never catch me getting that close to savage Indians.

When the hunters were all packed to leave, a passel of savages surrounded then and forced them to give them all their furs, skins, equipment, guns and horses. They told the hunters that if they ever returned, they would be killed.

Now I never had nary a bit of sympathy for these hunters. They should have known better than to trust Indians. Trusting Indians is like trusting copperheads. Copperheads are poison snakes and they bite. Indians are lying, thieving, snakes and they lie and steal.

You can damn well bet that Lige would never have trusted the savages and you can double damn bet that I wouldn't have trusted them.

Lige was full grown but mighty lean. I never saw him in a pair of breeches. He always wore a breechclout and tanned deerskin leggings. He wore a tanned deerskin hunting frock, even in summer. He said he didn't want to waste money on cloth when deerskin could be had so easy. When Lige wasn't barefoot, he wore moccasins. He kept his hair longer than shoulder length and shaved every month or so whether he needed shaving or not.

Lige carried a rifle from Lancaster, Pennsylvania and two of the biggest powder horns I had ever seen. Two tomahawks, two sheathed knives and a large shoulder pouch completed his outfit.

The story was told that Lige had been a real religious man from a Quaker family that had followed the Boones out of Pennsylvania to the Yadkin Valley. Lige had been regarded as a solid member of the Friends' group and dead set agin violence. This all changed during the French and Indian war. A neighboring family had been attacked and killed by the Cherokee. One of those killed was the woman Lige had intended to marry. Lige went wild after that and hadn't been back to a Friends meeting since. It was said that Lige had killed a sight of Indians, even after we were supposed to be at peace. When asked, Lige said that he didn't declare his war against the Indians but that he would decide if and when it was over.

Despite his woodsy habits, Lige was more educated than most of the men in western North Carolina. It was even said that he could read some Latin. First his mother, then a traveling preacher had taught him reading and sums. Because he showed an ability to learn, the traveling preacher persuaded Lige's parents to allow him to take him to Charles Town, in South Carolina, to get more schooling. It was rumored that Lige still packed books with him when he went into the woods. I later found that this was true.

There was one thing I didn't know about Lige. I didn't know why my pa could send for him and get him to come 'ready for travel.' I knew Lige and pa were friends but beyond that, I didn't know any particulars. I sure couldn't think of another time where anyone had been able to send for Lige and have him come ready for travel. I thought about asking Lige but he wasn't a man who invited questions. I decided I would wait and ask pa. It occurred to me that there might be more things I didn't know about pa.

Lige took the lead without asking me any questions or telling me anything. I started to tell him that I had already showed that I could handle a man-sized load in a fight but figured that could wait too.

I followed Lige while Bear roamed a little piece away from us, still fully alert. When we got to the cabin clearing, no one was in sight. Lige looked at Bear. Bear wasn't showing that he was disturbed so Lige let out a low clear whistle. An answering whistle came from our orchard and Amos stepped out. Before we had a chance to move into the clearing, Pa stepped up beside us.

He was so quiet and so quick that I was startled. Lige smiled at my reaction. I'm pretty sure that I had never seen him smile before.

Pa didn't waste any time. "It's time to go."

Lige motioned me to follow him. I looked at pa and he nodded.

"Take Bear with you."

I shifted the Brown Bess and followed Lige.

Lige set a pretty good pace and we covered a lot of ground. Sometimes he would point out a spot a quarter or half mile ahead and tell me to take Bear and cover one side of the trail and meet him there. We made twelve miles before we came to a small farm that was apparently our destination. Lige went up to the cabin and pounded on the door. Two rifles poked out of windows before the door opened. Lige talked to the man a few minutes.

I wasn't close enough to hear what was said but there was a lot of activity when they finished. Two half grown boys came out and fetched horses from a shed. They each lit out in different directions. The womenfolk in the house started stirring and I could tell food was being cooked. I didn't know who these folks were or why they were going to so much trouble for us.

Lige came over to where I rested with Bear. "I want you and Bear to hide out of sight. If there is anything amiss when I bring your pa to the clearing, I need you to warn us. If you can't do anything else, fire that double loaded musket of yours."

"It aint rightly mine, I took it from one of the Tory raiders."

"Well, it's yours now."

I was tired. I hadn't had any rest since I took the first watch the night before, and none before then since sun up. When I sat down, I started to doze off. I shook it off and started to move around. It took some doing but I stayed awake until Lige led pa and the others to the farm cabin. The farmer's sons and half a dozen armed men came in just a little later.

I helped unsaddle and unpack the horses. Pa gripped my shoulder. "You've put in quite a day's work, Aaron. Do you want food or sleep?"

"Both, I aint et and I can hardly stay awake."

Pa nodded and led me into the cabin. The farmer's wife gave me a bait of cornpone and fried side meat. I took the meal outside to eat. I saved part of it for Bear and drank about five gourds of water. I was beginning to feel more comfortable but I was still half asleep. Lige came over to me and led me back to the brush where I had been waiting before. "Keep Bear with you and get some sleep. Be careful and don't shoot any of the men who came here to guard your family." I think I was asleep before he walked away.

5

Indentured Servants

The sun woke me. Bear was guarding me. It took me a few minutes to remember where I was and what had happened to get me there. I moved out of the sun and back into the cool shade. I had taken the edge off my tiredness which was likely as good as it was going to get for a spell. I Bear was stretching and sniffing the air but he didn't show any excitement. I figured we were safe but I carried the Brown Bess as I went over to where a table had been set up under the shade of some oaks.

The meal was cured side meat and corn pone again but this time there was mush with wild honey and plenty of coffee to wash it down. I thanked the woman and it occurred to me that I didn't know her name to thank her proper but I was just a little too backward to ask and she didn't seem to mind.

I found a place to sit down where it looked like the shade wouldn't move for a spell and began my late breakfast. I wanted to feed some to

Bear but I didn't want to have the farmer and his wife thinking I was wasting the food they were giving us. I needn't have worried though. Lucy, Ben's sister fetched a pan of scraps that she set down for Bear. Bear waited until I told him before he started to eat.

Lige came up to share my shade. He tossed a scrap to Bear. Bear took the food from Lige. After he settled down, Lige said, "You did real good yesterday."

I thanked Lige and before I knew it, I was asking Lige how he and pa come to be friends. Lige took a long drink of water and began to tell me a tale I had never heard before.

I had known that pa and ma had come to North Carolina as indentured servants from Ulster, Ireland in 1756. What I didn't know was that Lige's folks owned their indenture. They were real lucky in that respect. Lige's folks were hardworking Quakers who expected everyone to work hard, but they were fair.

Indentured servants had few if any rights. One master could sell or swap their indenture to another man. . They could not vote. They had to get permission from their masters before they could get married or leave their houses. Without their master's permission, they could not buy or sell anything. Some masters relished the power their position gave them and would rape indentured women without any fear of punishment. Masters could punish indentured servants by almost any way they wanted to punish them. I had heard tales of masters of indentured servants beating them with a stick on the head and shoulders until the servant bled, and this for the least trifling mistake.

Most indentured servants were put to work in the tobacco fields or other field work. This was hard never ending work under the hot summer sun. The work was done from can-see in the morning until can't –see in the evening. Most indentured servants from England, Ireland, Scotland, Wales and the other countries across the water were not used to working under such hot conditions. The masters were sometimes good men who put an overseer in charge of the indentured servants. The overseers were often cruel, and mercilessly beat the servants to make them work faster and harder.

Some folks say that there was no difference between slaves and indentured servants. Sometimes there was a lot of difference and sometimes there was very little difference. The slave owner had a greater investment in his slaves. He might want to keep them healthy so that they can work for him longer. On the other hand, the indentured servant can be penalized by adding more time to his contract by the master. Both the slave and the indentured servant had to please the owner or suffer consequences. I can understand how to most folks the slaves appear to be more pitiful than indentured servants. The main reason for this is that slaves are not given freedom, no matter how long they work. Slaves are property of their owner for as long as they live. Now I have heard of some folks freeing their slaves in their will but this don't happen often.

The life of an indentured servant could be good or at least bearable. The life of an indentured servant could also be very harsh and even unbearable. The comfort of an indentured servant depended on the will of their master. Some masters thought all indentured servants were criminals and debtors. This was sometimes true but many indentured servants were like my pa and ma, people looking for a better life than what they could get in Ireland. Most indentured servants arrived without a penny in their pockets and had to accept the master they got, no matter how hard the master was to work for. Most of the indentured servants came from very little and while they were still indentured, they had little if any more. Sometimes they had less.

Indentured servants had been in England and Ireland about a hundred years. Many people in Ireland were referred to as Scotch-Irish because they were moved to Ireland. Sometimes they were moved to get them out of Scotland and sometimes they were moved to dilute the effect of the Irish in a region of Ireland. Sometimes they were moved for both reasons.

The men and women in Ireland had a great incentive to immigrate to the colonies. At the time my pa and ma immigrated, the common people in Ireland owned less than ten percent of the property. My pa and ma wanted to own land and be beholden to no one. Only by immigrating to the colonies was there any chance to own property and gain some independence.

Indentured servants can be given freedom after they have finished their contract. Now a seven year contract can be extended. Pa and Ma agreed to a contract for eight years so they wouldn't be separated. Days, months or even years can be added to contracts for any number of real or imagined mistakes. If the servant is contracted to receive three shirts and two pairs of breeches a year, any clothing beyond that can be charged to the servant. The master can be as fair or as unfair as his conscience allows him to be.

When the contract has been fulfilled, the servant has liberty to go and do what he chooses. Some masters give the servant a stake of money and goods to get started. This is called freedom dues. After they are freed from the contract, the freed servant can either set up their own business or take a job with someone else. It should be remembered that this freedom aint a guarantee. Freedom can be delayed if the any part of the agreement is proved to have been violated. Because of this, an indentured servant's indentured years can be extended to as long as the master says it needs to be extended.

I always knew that pa and ma were grateful to the masters they had served. I didn't know until I talked to Lige that he and what was left of his family were just as grateful to pa and ma. When the Cherokee trouble hit the Yadkin Valley, Lige said pa saved his family. Lige made a point of telling me that both he and the farmer who was keeping us owed pa their lives. In fact, Lige told me that a lot of other men owed pa for saving their lives.

"Well why," I asked Lige, "If so many men owe pa their lives, does pa want to leave."

Lige was quiet for a minute or two, then he told me, "Some of the men who owe your pa side with the king now. Your pa don't want to fight men he once fought beside."

6

INDIAN WAR

Lige closed his eyes as he told me about pa. Looking back, I'm not sure he could have told me while looking at me. He still carried a sight of pain twenty years later than the story he told me. The way I understood it, the British and the French had been fighting to get full control of the whole continent. There had been wars going back since before 1700. Both sides tried to bribe the Indians to help their side by attacking the other side's settlements. In 1754, there were skirmishes that led to there being a full scale war. In the colonies, this war called the French and Indian war and I understand it was called the Seven Years War in Europe. That was beyond our concern in North Carolina. We called it the Cherokee War. I don't know that I ever heard what the Cherokee called it. If I ever did hear what the Cherokee called it, I've forgotten.

The Cherokee claimed they killed people in North Carolina to avenge the killing of Cherokee men up in Virginia. I don't know if that was the truth but it was what they said. When the killing started in both western South Carolina and western North Carolina, the Governor of South Carolina, William Henry Lyttleton, organized approximately one thousand men and marched into the backcountry of South Carolina in the fall of 1759. Lige let me know that as a member of the Society of Friends, a Quaker, he was not one of that force.

Lige didn't miss much when he missed out on joining Lyttleton's force. Lyttleton caught up with the Cherokee and only a river separated the two forces. While they waited, men in Lyttleton's force began to show symptoms of smallpox and they returned to Charles Town before it could weaken the force so much that the Cherokee could defeat them. Unfortunately, after they returned to Charles Town, they spread the smallpox to the people there.

Settlers were still on the lookout for trouble but were gradually growing less watchful. There were bands roving to try to stop any Indian raids but they weren't well organized.

Lige wasn't a part of any of the bands of men who scouted the area around the Yadkin Valley. In fact, Lige admitted that at the time he had felt sorry for men who could be turned warlike in such a hurry. He had made up his mind that he would not do anything to threaten another man. He could think of nothing that could come close to changing his mind. Nothing, until he and pa were taking care of the stock one morning.

Lige remembered that it was a morning no different from any other. They were just getting started when pa grabbed his arm and pointed to the west. There, instead of a comfortable feather of smoke rising above the forest, was rolling waves of smoke. Lige ran to the house to rouse everyone, thinking there was just a house afire. Lige grabbed a plow horse and had already started when two men came running up. The men were scared and out of breath. They were able to say one word, "Injuns."

Lige had already left. His ma came running up to pa and said, "John Burns, thee must help Elijah."

Now she only meant that pa should go and fetch Lige back, but pa didn't take it that way. He grabbed up a double bitted ax and lit out after Lige. He cut across the woods and field and reached the spot of the massacre at the same time Lige got there.

Lige was all tore up and for a spell he just stood there. Two Cherokee grabbed him and one had raised a club when pa came up swinging the double bitted axe and hollering "Erin go Brae." That was the minute that Lige fell out with the Society of Friends. He saw where the woman he loved and her family had been murdered while unarmed and he went crazy. Lige admitted that as much as he tried, he didn't accomplish much. He was strong and he sure wanted to kill the lot of them but he had never even been in a wrestling match before.

Pa had been in plenty of fights and he had seen plenty of fights. Most of all, pa wanted to survive. He didn't aim to die a bound man, as indentured servants were called. At first the Indians tried to attack him but his long arms swinging the sharp double bitted axe was cutting through muscle and bone. Some attackers lost arms and legs before they died. The Indians decided he was too crazy to kill and figured leaving was a good idea. The trouble was, both pa and Lige chased them.

Lige caught one and shook him, shouting, "Does thee know what thee hast done? Does thee know what thee hast done? Does thee know what thee hast done? Does thee know what thee hast done?"

Three turned back to help their captured friend and pa killed them with the axe. Pa used the axe handle to knock Lige's captive senseless and tended to Lige. Lige told me that he was more than half crazy. He wanted to keep running after the fleeing Cherokee and make them listen to how bad they had been. Pa kept him there until other men came to help them.

Lige's pa and the other neighbors were shocked as much at the Indians pa had hewn all to hell with the axe as they were at the massacred bodies of their neighbors.   Pa was covered with Indian blood and Lige was none too clean. The men dug four graves. The settlers were placed in three and all the Indians and their cut off arms and legs were thrown in the fourth grave.

When the Indian woke up from the axe handle sleep, he made the mistake of not showing that he was sorry for helping kill the woman Lige loved and her family. Filled with grief, Lige hit him so hard that the Indian died. Lige said that was the only Indian he killed that he hadn't intended to kill. Every Indian that he killed after that was intentional. Lige also said there were plenty of Indians killed by him after that.

To the disappointment of his family, Lige let his family know that he was going to join the expedition against the Cherokee. Despite their attempts to reason with him, Lige made sure they knew he was going with or without their approval. His ma finally turned to his pa and said, "Elijah must take John Burns with him."

Both approached pa. Lige's pa spoke first, "John Burns, thee must go with Elijah and try to bring him home safe."

For maybe the only time in her life, Lige's ma interrupted her husband. "John Burns," she said, "If thee brings my son home safely, thee will have a farm at the end of thy servitude." "And if," she continued, "thee is killed, thy wife and child will be provided for."

Pa turned to Mr. Black and said, "I'll need weapons."

Mr. Black didn't answer right off but Mrs. Black did. "Yes, thee must go to Blake's and tell him to give thee and Elijah what thee needs. Tell him my husband will take care of the costs."

When he told me this, Lige smiled one of his few smiles and said he thought his pa was going to choke when he heard what his wife said. Lige said that he and pa went to Blake's where they got armed and provisioned. While they were there, they learned that the Cherokees had committed further attacks on white settlers. The News had just reached Blake's that group of refugees whose wagons were mired in a swamp near Long Cane Creek had been massacred. Blake advised Lige and pa to wait for a bigger expedition to be organized. Pa counseled patience and told Lige that while they waited, they could practice marksmanship and fighting skills. For two months, they worked all day and practiced every evening.

Soon, they learned that a second campaign was being organized. This campaign was to be led by Colonel Archibald Montgomery. Montgomery seemed to know what he was doing. By moving swiftly into the backcountry, they surprised the Cherokee. Using this surprise to their advantage, they completely destroyed the lower towns of the Cherokee Nation. Montgomery continued until his force was ambushed by the Cherokee near Echoe. The ambush happened as they as they passed through the mountains along the Little Tennessee River. Montgomery, having lost the element of surprise retreated back to Charles Town.

The following year, Lige and pa joined a force led by Colonel James Grant. Grant had been Montgomery's second in command. He hadn't forgotten Montgomery's successes or that they had been ambushed. Grant's force spent over a month destroying the lower and middle towns of the Cherokee. Grant's force burned the Cherokee towns and crops and generally raised hell. Grant then returned to Charles Town. That September, a delegation of the Cherokee asked for peace and treaties were signed.

Pa returned to the Black farm to complete his indenture but Lige felt he could not return. He virtually lived in the woods and it was rumored that he continued to kill Indians. Lige never did tell me if any of the rumors were true.

Lige did tell me that my pa was a fighting fool. Lige said it wasn't because pa liked killing but because he didn't want to be killed. Pa, he said, just wanted to make sure he returned to the woman and family that he loved. He also said that the number of men who owed their life to pa's protection couldn't be counted on two hands.

7

LEGEND AND FACT

I took a while to think on what Lige had told me. I had never considered pa to be a fearsome man. A strong man, a firm and steady man, a man who worked hard for his family but I had never considered pa to be a fierce or fearsome man. I tried to imagine him as a hell on wheels fighting man and I couldn't. Then I remembered the six men armed with rifles or muskets that had been killed with a knife or a tomahawk around our cabin. I reckoned finally that there was a side to pa that I had never seen before.

I got up and stretched. I walked to pa and asked what I should be doing. I wasn't used to resting during daylight and allowed that there was something that needed my attention.

Pa thought a minute and motioned for me to follow him. He took me to the farmer and said, "Aaron, this is Gabriel Davis."

I took the work calloused hand that was offered and shook it.

Pa continued, "Gabriel, this is my son Aaron, he's getting restless and wants to know what you need for him to be doing."

Gabriel seemed just a little startled at the offer but he was pleased to get the offer of help. He thought about the offer and said, "John, if he's up to it, he can help by sons and daughters with the garden. That'll keep him close. I know he's able to do a lot more but I figured you'd want him kept close."

Pa nodded and called out, "Moses, Samuel, come here."

Moses and Samuel came running over. Both had picked up a rifle, pouch and powder horn first. Pa seemed to approve that all of us were armed. Even Gabriel Davis seemed to approve.

"Gabriel needs some help with his garden. Keep your weapons handy and help his sons with their garden. They'll know what needs doing so you all do it."

Moses and Samuel seemed to feel a little let down to come all ready for man-sized action and be put to garden work. But pa said it so we did it. We walked to where over an acre of garden was protected from large animas by a rail fence and leaned our weapons against the fence. We hung our pouches and powder horns next to them and took hoes to where Gabriel Davis' three sons and one of his daughters were planting corn, beans and squash in long straight rows.

We set right to work and got going at a pretty good clip. We were doing three rows at a time. After an hour, one of the boys sent his sister to fetch a bucket of water and a gourd dipper. He waited until his sister was out of hearing and turned to face us.

"Is it true that your pa is John Burns?"

Moses and Samuel were some startled by the question and I would have been too if Lige hadn't filled me in on Pa's past and his reputation. As it was, neither Moses nor Samuel knew why anyone would ask the question. Before they had a chance to take offence, I answered.

"Yes, our pa is John Burns."

"Wow! We've heard about him all of our lives."

By now both Moses and Samuel knew that they weren't being insulted but they still had no idea why the Davis boys were so impressed. The older boy, about eighteen years old asked, "Do you know what my whole name is?"

Samuel was the first to answer, "No I don't reckon we do."

The oldest boy, or I guess I should say young man stood up straight and tall and answered, "John Burns Davis."

Now it's a sure fact that Moses, Samuel and me were all some surprised. Me maybe not as much because Lige had already let me in on pa's past. Moses and Samuel just stared.

Samuel finally asked, "Are we kin."

"Don't reckon."

"Then how'd you come to have my pa's name?"

"Your pa saved my pa's life way back yonder in the Indian wars."

Moses and Samuel had the same expression I probably had when Lige told me that my pa was a fighter in the Indian wars. It was hard to believe that the man we had known all of our lives could be a well-known Indian fighter.

Now we all knew that Lige was an Indian fighter. Most people figured he had never stopped fighting Indians. Knowing what I knew about Lige losing the woman he planned to marry to an Indian raid, I could understand Lige's point of view on the subject of Killing Indians.

But Lige was different from pa. Lige dressed in tanned buckskin. Lige usually wore a breechclout and leggings. Liger could be gone for weeks at a time. Lige did not even keep a permanent home or cabin, even though I now knew he could easily have done so.

Pa was a farmer. A farmer no different from most other farmers. He had rarely left the farm. Now we were being told that a lot of other people on the North Carolina frontier knew things about our pa that we had never even thought about.

I learned much later that deeds a little above and beyond the ordinary could be stretched far beyond any resemblance to actual fact. As a lad of fourteen, I was still not ready to abandon the image of the pa I had known all of my life to the pa that grateful men named their sons after. It was that much harder for Moses, Samuel and me because pa had never told us any tales about Indian fighting.

Some things were slowly beginning to make sense. The time when we had dinner on the ground when a circuit riding preacher came through. Some folks come from as far as fifteen miles away and travelers who learned of the preaching and dinner on the grounds. Made their way to the church meeting. One of the men who stopped long enough for church and dinner began swapping tales of fighting Indians with four other men. Two of the men were local farmers and the other two were traveling.

The talk began to get boastful and loud. Their language began to be profane. Women were beginning to move their children when the circuit riding preacher came over to pa and two other farmers. The circuit riding preacher led them to the braggarts and said to them, "I thought you might like to meet John Burns."

The three travelers appeared to suddenly remember they needed to get back to traveling. The two farmers, suddenly a little shame-faced, went back to their families.

We had never heard pa brag. We had never seen pa so drunk that he couldn't handle himself. I don't think we had ever seen pa lose his temper. Now, for the first time in our lives, we were hearing tales told about pa that we had never imagined could be about our pa.

Keeping a garden on the frontier was important. In the late spring, summer and early fall folks got fresh food from gardens. After the first killing freeze, or after the growing season ended, folks relied on dried vegetables or vegetables that could be kept in a root cellar to provide food to go with the fresh and cured meat they butchered. Potatoes, squash, yams and pumpkins were kept in root cellars. Folks dried beans, peas, slices of pumpkins and apples for the winter as well. Sometimes folks pickled beans, corn and cucumbers for winter eating.

The beans, corn and squash we were planting were just one of the plantings that would be done during the summer. Fresh beans, corn and squash were already available. Another crop would be ready in about two weeks and at least one more crop would be planted. Folks that planted this way got to eat a lot of fresh garden food.

The garden work went quickly. About an hour before dark, we finished and put our hoes away. We had just washed up at the creek so we could go to supper when one of the men who had come when called the night before rode into the clearing.

The rider tied his horse close enough to the water trough for it to drink and hurried to where pa, Lige and Mr. Davis were talking. I decided that supper could wait and drifted over behind pa and settled down to listen.

"John," the rider was saying, "you can't let this stand. Your reputation will be smeared and blackguarded."

Pa didn't say anything. He kept flipping his knife into a fence rail, walking over to get his knife and continued flipping the knife. I could tell that pa was considering all the parts of the problem and would make up his mind soon.

"John," the rider practically begged, "all of us who helped you will be tarred by the same brush as you are."

8

WOLF HEAD TAVERN

Pa stood and nodded. "You're right, there's no reason for you to be hurt because of anything I done."

Without another word, pa went over to where the horses were tied and bridled his horse. He then placed his saddle on the back of his own horse. While he was getting his saddle cinched I asked John Burns Davis what was going on.

John Burns Davis was so excited that he had trouble keeping still. It took him a minute or two to settle down and tell me, and Lige who had just come up behind me, what was going on.

"Zack was over to the Wolf Head Tavern. He said that Jason Smith is over there spreading a whole bunch of lies about your pa. Jason Smith is telling everyone that your pa took them men prisoner. He says that the men had surrendered and been tied up. He claims that after they were tied up, that your pa murdered them with his knife."

By the time John Burns Davis had finished speaking, Lige was on his way to the horses and I was right behind him. Lige motioned to two other men and they joined us. By the time we reached the horses, Moses had joined us.

We bridled and saddled the horses we were going to ride, picked up our weapons, pouches and powder horns and followed Lige. About four miles later, we rounded a curve in time to see pa step into a large two level cabin.

The Wolf Head Tavern was a business with many purposes. It sold food and drink to travelers and local people. It also sold sleeping space to people with the need for it and the coin to pay for it. It was large. It measured fourteen by twenty-eight feet and had a second floor, not just a sleeping attic. A covered dogtrot connected the cabin to a kitchen that was only about nine by eleven feet. This prevented the main cabin from getting too hot when meals were prepared. The first floor of the cabin was a single room. The main feature was a twelve foot bar with barrels of spirits stacked behind it. A long table with benches on either side was permanently place to feed travelers. The table was used whether there was two travelers or twenty travelers.

A large fireplace was at each end of the building. There was no fire in either now but when cool weather hit, both would be roaring. There was only smoke from the kitchen cabin as we rode up to the door.

"Moses," Lige stated, take care of all the horses."

Now I could see that Moses was wanting to object because, after all, I was the youngest. He wanted to object but something in Lige's voice told him it wouldn't be wise. Lige got to the door and motioned for us to slow down. He side stepped to the right side of the door and I side stepped to the left side. I found that I was standing beside pa.

Pa raised his finger to his lips as the other two entered. There were eleven other men in the building, not counting the publican who was behind the bar. Jason Smith was waxing oratorical, which is to say Jason Smith was lying his head off. Four men were apparently with Jason Smith. The others were travelers.

"It happened just like I said, John Burns tricked ten men into surrendering. He promised them they would be released and could return to their families. He waited until they were tied up. Then he took his knife and he murdered them."

He took a long swallow of ale and continued, "I saw it all and couldn't do anything about it."

One of the older travelers, a man of about fifty years old, asked, "Jason, are you sure? This don't sound like the John Burns that I knew"

"Are you calling me a liar?"

"I just said that it don't sound like the John Burns I knew."

"Well that sounds to me like you are calling me a liar. I don't put up with being called a liar."

I started to step forward but pa placed his hand in front of me. He shook his head and motioned me back.

"Anybody wants to call me a liar, just call away.   Then him and me will go outside and settle it. Just him and me. Fists, guns, or knives."

The older travel stood.   Two other men tried to keep him from standing. He pushed their hands away and stood.

"I stand by what I said. I knew John Burns. He saved my life and the lives of a whole lot of other people. What you accuse him of sure don't sound like John Burns."

"So you're calling me a liar?"

"Well, if I got the choice of backing down or calling you a liar or backing down," he hesitated for effect. "Then," he continued, "You're a damn liar."

Despite having offered the options of going outside to settle the matter with fist, knife, or gun; Jason picked up his musket."

Pa stepped forward, reaching Jason in three steps. He grabbed Jason's musket with his right hand and Jason with his left. Jerking the musket away from Jason, he shoved Jason into the men with him.

"Jason," pa roared out, "I call you a liar."

For about half a minute, there was not a sound. Then I heard the soft click of a flintlock being cocked. From the location of the sound, I knew it was either Lige or one of the men beside him. I cocked mine too. I wasn't sure what would happen next but I felt better when Lige spoke.

"Let's just keep this between the two of them. There aint no use in all of us getting killed. Everybody stay out of it. Don't anybody else interfere."

The older traveler was still standing. He broke the tension by asking, "Is that you Lige?"

"It's me Will."

"Is that John with you?"

Lige didn't want to tell what he knew so he answered, "Will, there's five of us."

"If it's all right with you, I'd like to stand beside you and keep things peaceful."

"I'd like that, Will."

Will stepped toward Lige. "If it's all right, I can remove weapons from Jason and his friends."

"Do it without getting in my line of fire."

Will carefully moved to the men at the bar. He first took all the weapons that he could see. Then he felt the men's clothing and removed three knives. While there, he looked straight into pa's face and grinned a great big grin.

"Hello John," he whispered.

"Howdy Will, it's been a long time."

Pa shoved Jason down so that Jason was sitting with his back against the bar. Lige stepped up with his cocked weapon pointed up. I moved up when Lige moved.

Pa turned to face the publican behind the bar and said, "Light a lamp."

As soon as the candle was lit and placed in a lantern, pa shifted so he could face more of the men in the tavern.

"Men, I am John Burns. Jason is a damn liar. I'm not mad at any of you and I'll try to answer any concerns and questions you have."

For about a minute, no one spoke. Then one man stepped up with his hands open. "Did you kill ten men after they surrendered?"

"No. I was waiting in the dark when my cabin was surrounded. Jason Smith hallooed my cabin while his men waited to ambush anyone who came out. When the firing started, I used a knife and a tomahawk to fight with. No one tried to surrender and I didn't ask anyone to surrender. Every man I killed was armed with a firelock. Jason Smith is a damn liar."

Will spoke up. "Men, I served with John during the Indian wars. This sounds like the John Burns I served with."

Will turned to a younger man of about seventeen years old. "Nathan, your pa was with us. You were born after we got back. If it wasn't for John Burns, you would never have seen your pa."

"Yes, my pa told me about it," Nathan told the crowd.

Pa spoke directly to Jason, "Jason, you gave people the choice of fists, guns, or knives. I offer you another choice. Leave. Leave and if I ever hear of you lying about me again, I'll kill you. If I ever see you again and even suspect you mean me or mine harm, I'll kill you. Make your choice."

Jason said nothing.

"Choose!"

Pa spoke so loudly that I jumped.

"I'll leave."

Jason slowly stood and reached for his firelock.

"No." Lige spoke sharply and clearly.

"No man," Lige continued, "that would ambush a man and his family at night will go into the darkness armed."

Jason motioned for his friends to follow him. I followed them out of the tavern. I heard Lige fall in behind me.

I had forgotten that Moses was outside with the horses. Moses had no way of knowing what was happening inside. He had just heard pa yell 'choose,' and now he was watching Jason Smith and four friends leave the tavern.

Jason whispered something to his friends and two of them grabbed Moses and wrested his rifle away. Jason and the other two went for the horses. I fired almost before I thought and heard the boom of Lige's rifle beside me. My shot got one of the men who had grabbed Moses and Lige's shot had taken down one of the men trying to steal the horses. Moses, with only one man to deal with, was all right. He got the Tory in a chokehold and did not let go.

It looked for a short spell like the other two might get away with all or some of the horses. Then Lige and I were reinforced by a growling mass of brown fur, muscle, teeth and mad as hell dog. I should have known Bear would follow us to the tavern.

Bear got one Tory by the leg and didn't let go. The Tory came off the horse and all the horses commenced a bucking. I guess they were scared more by Bear's growling attack than they had been scared by the gunfire. Lige swung a tomahawk at a tory who was going back to help the one that Moses had in a chokehold, hitting him with the poll of the tomahawk and knocking him cold. Both of us grabbed for Jason Smith as he tried to mount a bucking, scared horse.

All this had only taken a minute and by now the Tavern had emptied and everyone, including the publican was outside. Pa took a good look and asked Jason, "I thought you chose to leave, didn't you?"

Jason was silent. Pa leaned his rifle, pouch and powder horn against the hitch rail. He then took off his knife and tomahawk and handed them to Will.

Moses still had the Tory in a choke hold. Pa went over to them and said, "Give him some air."

Moses loosened his hold and the Tory first gasped and then began to suck in great gulps of air. Moses still had a good hold on him. Pa walked over and looked at him.

"Do you want to tell everyone here what happened?"

The Tory tried to speak but couldn't yet so he just nodded.

Speaking just loud enough for everyone to hear him, pa asked, "Will you tell everyone here what happened?"

The Tory nodded and choked out, "yes."

"Then start talking."

"When we came out, Jase told me and Tim to grab the horse guard and take his rifle and all his weapons while he and the others got the horses."

Pa turned to the tavern crowd and asked, "Is there anyone here who don't know what happened?"

Will spoke, "We know, John."

Pa walked over to Jason Smith and said, "Fists."

Jason must have thought that grappling pa and putting him down was a good strategy because that is what he tried to do. The grapple was a common way of fighting on the frontier. Pa was ready for his move and stepped back and to the side. As Jason went by, he grabbed him by the hair of the head and hauled him back. The pa commenced to take him to school.

I don't know as I have ever seen a man get a worse whipping that that Tory got. Pa held him by the hair of the head and hit him several times in the gut. Then he worked on his face. Finally, he pushed Jason down on the wood pile and turned back to check on Moses.

Pa thought he had beat Jason enough to settle things and that would have been it, but Jason grabbed the axe from the wood pile and ran at pa while his back was turned. I yelled and most of the others yelled too. Pa turned and grabbed the axe handle. Using the force of Jason's rush against him, Pa wound up with the axe. Holding the axe handle close to the blade, pa swung the handle as hard as he could at Jason. Jason raised his arms to try to catch the blow. We all heard the snap as the axe handle broke the bone in Jason's left forearm.

Jason screamed and fell in a sitting position. While he screamed, Pa went to the well and pulled up a bucket of water. He emptied the bucket of water over his head and drew a second bucket. This time he got the gourd dipper and drank three gourd dippers of water.

He went over to where Jason and his four friends were sitting and told them, "If I see you again soon, it will be bad for you."

We mounted and left the tavern. Will came with us.

Pa never looked back.

I never heard it told again that Pa had murdered prisoners. If I had heard it and he wouldn't kill the liars who were spreading such lies about him, then I would have killed them.

It took me a long time to understand that pa didn't give a damn what anyone said. He figured that the people who knew him would know the truth and strangers didn't matter none. The only reason he went to the tavern to straighten out Jason Smith was because he didn't want any loose talk about the friends who were helping him.

Even when I understood pa's thinking on it, it wouldn't have stopped me. If I'd heard of anybody spreading lies about pa, either me or that person would have died.

9

MARTIN'S STATION

I hadn't heard a lot about Martin's station before we got there but I have learned a lot since. The station, which started out like most stations did with a few cabins surrounded by a pole stockade, was first built in the late 1760's by Joseph Martin. Martin was a young, adventurous man from Albemarle County, Virginia. He served in the Virginia Militia under George Washington during the French and Indian War. He knew or met Dr. Thomas Walker who later hired Martin to lead an expedition into Powell's Valley to help protect his land claims there. Martin was promised 21,000 acres to make sure he was the first to settle there. Martin barely arrived ahead of another group bent on settling there.

It was not only hard getting to the land, building a station and settling there, he had the cursed savages to deal with. Cherokee Indians came down on Martin's Station like a swarm of bees. This forced him to abandon his station and return to Albemarle County. In 1775, Martin and around twenty men returned to Powell's Valley and built a semi-permanent station. This time he built cabins to live in surrounded by a stronger stockade. This station was the last many travelers saw before crossing through the Cumberland Gap and into Kentucky.

Because the settling of Kentucky started getting serious in 1775 after Judge Richard Henderson's treaty with the Cherokee at the Sycamore Shoals, settlement was hindered by the war with the damned British. The British figured, I guess, that the more they hired the red dogs to fight for them, the more distracted the

Continental army would be. From the beginning of the war until the end of the war we just finished where General Andy Jackson whipped hell out of the British at N 'Orleans, the bloody British hired the cursed red dogs to attack the frontier settlements. Now the part of the war fought east of the mountains got all the attention but those of us on the frontier damn sure got our share of it.

Pa didn't mind fighting the savage Indians. He said they weren't any kin and they weren't his neighbors. They were just dogs sicced on us by the British. I reckon pa was right. Damn straight we frontiersmen held our own.

Daniel Boone had been hired by Judge Richard Henderson to build a trace connecting Martin's Station, through the Cumberland Gap and into Kentucky. I have heard some folks refer to this as the Wilderness Road but back then there was no road about it. They didn't start building the Wilderness Road until 1796. You could walk over it, ride a horse over it, and even drive some stock over it. But there was no way that a wagon could be taken over it. By my way of thinking, you couldn't call it a road as long as you had to clear briars and brush. That, and I didn't figure it was a road until a wagon could be pulled over it. Boone's Trace was just that, a trace through the wilderness. Two or three years of not being used and the wilderness would swaller up the trace like it had never been there.

Getting back to the worthless, greedy, bloodthirsty British; they had a lot of reasons for wanting us kept east of the mountains. It would have tickled them to death to have the United States confined to a narrow strip between the Atlantic Ocean and the mountains. That would have left them everything south of Canada and east of the Mississippi River. That and they would soon have pushed Spain out and got everything west of the Appalachians and east of the Pacific Ocean. There aint nothing I would put past those worthless, hell-bound redcoats.

We were all glad to reach Martin's Station. For one thing, maybe pa would stop posting guards while we were there. It wasn't just the guard duty. As I had learned, it was easy for a tired man to doze off on guard duty. Pa would get up three or four times of a night and check the men on guard. He only had to catch them asleep once for them to know that he wasn't pleased. Guard duty where a man couldn't catch some sleep wasn't their idea of a good job.

Martin's Station was better known to a lot of people than it was to me. I don't know how many people passed through going west put there was a passel of them. The wild country west of Moccasin Gap all the way west had more hostile savages than a dirty dog has fleas. This may be a bad way to compare them because the fleas probably had more worth than the hostile savages.

A lot of folks who don't know any better will claim that the savages were just fighting to protect their hunting grounds. I believe that is a damn lie. They were fighting because the British paid them to fight. I don't like them. I don't like the British or the Indians. If I found that I come down with the smallpox, I'd go to the biggest group of Indians that I could find and get in amongst them.

We rested at Martin's station. Our way hadn't been easy and it was about to get harder. Despite the hardships we knew were coming, we were all excited. There were six families and three unattached men in the party now. Everyone claimed they just wanted to get away from the neighbor fighting neighbor situation in North Carolina but I had suspicions that two of the families were running from debts. I figured that was their lookout and not mine. There had been seven families. The seventh family was the Johnson family. The old man and his two sons had bucked against pa on guard duty and other camp duties.

They bucked and pa let them know that they weren't wanted. "Go your own way," he told them.

"You can't stop us from going into Kentucky."

"No, but I can stop you from going with us."

"You can't stop us from camping next to you."

"I wouldn't try to stop you. You'll stop you."

The man was obviously puzzled by pa's statement but he didn't ask what pa meant. I was some puzzled too but I didn't want to let on so I kept my mouth shut. Days later, I did ask pa what he meant.

"Aaron, they were a family of leeches. They were like fleas on a dog. If a dog gets shut of its fleas, the fleas will find another dog that is easier to stay attached with. You can't always judge people by the way they look. The Johnson family looked lazy and sorry.

They were lazier and sorrier than they looked."

The next morning, we left at our usual time. The other family wasn't ready to move and pa ignored them. That day we traveled over an hour longer than usual. Lige had told us of a better camping place. He, along with Moses and Samuel had ridden ahead to build cooking fires and get the camp site ready. After that, we never saw or heard about that family again.

I never forgot what pa had to say about the Johnson family. I studied about it a right smart and finally decided that most folks do their best to hide their worst qualities. Time and time again, people have proven to me to be worse than I would have thought them to be. All except for the Indians and the British. Sometimes those sorry sons of bitches turn out to be not quite as terrible as I had them pegged to be. I guess a few of the British and Indians are sometimes halfway decent.

Joseph Martin himself greeted us with his right hand out ready to be shook.

"I'm Joseph Martin. Welcome to my station. You can camp on that flat spot there."

Pa shook his hand and said, "I'm John Burns. We are on our way into Kentucky."

Joseph Martin was a little startled. "Could you be the John Burns I have heard so much about?"

"I don't know."

Joseph Martin, seeing that pa was not going to give him any more information, started to turn away. That was when we heard Lige holler out, "Joe!"

Martin turned toward the sound of Lige's voice and hollered back, "Lige!"

"Joe Martin, you old bear, meet the man I've bragged on so much. This here is John Burns."

"John," Martin said, "I thought, from the way Lige talked, that you would be ten feet tall."

"Lige has been known to spin yarns."

"Then so have fifty or a hundred other men," Martin pointed out. "Now let's go sample a little of the rum I just got in."

Martin, Pa and Lige went inside the stockade. The women commenced to make things comfortable. Pa had already told them we would stay a little longer than we usually stayed on a stop. Yep. I don't know who first said that Martin's Station was a refuge in the wilderness but I have to agree with them. Martin's Station was about twenty miles east of Cumberland Gap. It was the last refuge in Virginia before entering Kentucky. It was the only place for several days journey where travelers could get some rest and resupply if need be. I wasn't familiar with Martin's Station before we got there but I was sure grateful for it when we did get there.

Martin Station was built where the trail crossed a creek. There was a spring inside the stockade so water would always be available. I learned firsthand how important this was when we were inside Bryant's Station.

Martin's Station. Photograph by Jim Cummings

10

CUMBERLAND GAP

Cherokee, Shawnee and warriors of other tribes had crossed through the Cumberland Gap for years. We called the path they used the warriors path because the Indians used it to make raids on each other. Lige said the Indians called it the Athowominee, or the "Path of the Armed Ones." As much as the Indians raided against each other, it seems they could have just killed each other off and saved us the trouble.

I couldn't wait to get to Cumberland Gap. A gap or gate through the mountains that men had heard of and searched for a long time. I have been told that Doctor Thomas Walker was the first white man to discover and name the Cumberland Gap. I don't know if that is true but it is what I have been told. Of course the Indians could have told us but you can never trust an Indian.

Cumberland Gap is important because it provides an easier way west than climbing over the mountains. The mountains have been a fence that prevented the movement of both animals and people. There were rumors of the gap going back over a hundred years. Indians knew where it was at but they don't tell all they know and I wouldn't trust one anyway.

The Appalachian Mountains were a fence that kept both animals and white men from traveling in an east to west or west to east direction. I have been told that there are three gaps where people can move in an east west direction but Cumberland Gap is the only one I have been through.

As we got to the gap, I was so excited I couldn't sit still. I wanted to run, shouting through the gap and into Kentucky. I didn't though. It would have shamed pa if I had acted like that.

Moses and Samuel were excited too. A month before, we had been on a farm in North Carolina. Now we were going through Cumberland Gap just like experienced woodsmen. We felt like experienced woodsmen too. I saw Lige nudge pa with his elbow as they watched us.

"Moses, are we in Kentucky yet?" Samuel was fairly hopping as he asked the question.

"I don't know. Samuel paused, "if we aint then we soon will be."

"Steady, people," pa ordered. We aint safe yet. "Steady."

I could just feel the excitement in all the people in our party. You would have thought we were at the end of our journey with a big house and a big dinner waiting for them. Never mind that it was still morning and we had only traveled about two hours since breaking camp. Never mind that we had just departed Martin's Station the morning before. Everyone figured that reaching Cumberland Gap was the amen to the prayer.

"Steady," pa reminded everyone.

"Steady," Lige echoed pa's reminder.
Ben came up to me and bumped his shoulder into mine. His

face was red and bright he was so excited. "Kentucky," Ben whispered.

"Steady," I whispered back.

I really wanted to let loose and holler but in a low voice, I reminded those around me, "steady."

A boy about mine and Ben's age decided to let loose. With a holler, be began running through grass and over rocks.

"Nate," pa told the boy's father, "settle him down."

"John, he's just a boy."

"Nate, settle him down." This time pa's voice had a crack in it, like a whip used on a yoke of oxen.

"Brian!"

That was as far as Nate got. A scream from Brian caused us to stop and every man to grab his rifle. Pa, Lige and Nate ran over to where Brian lay screaming.

I can still remember the sound of his screaming to this day. He was my age and he was screaming like a bee stung three year old that had run into a hornet nest. I saw Lige and pa hitting the ground with the butt of their rifles and then swing their tomahawks. Nate was carrying Brian back to where his ma was screaming a long keening wail. From where I was, I could see that he had been snake bit in both legs. I later found that he had been bit twice in one leg and three times in the other.

The women and his pa and Lige tried to help him but there was too much poison in him. He was dead within two hours. He was buried with a service an hour after that. It didn't seem real to me. It was more like a bad dream.

My ma and the other women tried to comfort Brian's ma. She didn't want to leave the grave and they gently coaxed her along. Nate was grieving silently but I could tell that he was in bad shape too. Come to think of it, I wasn't in the best shape I had ever been in either.

Brian was not a bad person or a disobedient boy. He just got excited and let loose in the wrong place at the wrong time. I guess we all learned right then that the Boone Trace and Kentucky, while wonderful, could be unforgiving.

Later Lige told me they had killed six copperheads in the area where Brian was bitten. That's the reason that today I hate copperheads almost as much as I hate the British and the Indians.

We moved on. Pa didn't have to say 'steady' now. Everyone knew what could happen if they weren't 'steady.' If anyone forgot, Brian's ma reminded them with her soft crying each night.

Pa made a change to guard duty after that. He had me and Bear guard part of every night.   He had me sit with my back to a tree or rock with Bear beside me.

"Trust Bear," pa said. "If Bear says there is danger, then there is probably danger."

I agreed with pa. I allowed that Bear was as sharp a dog as I would ever have. The extra guard duty cut into my sleep some but I figured that I could take it. The hardest part of guard duty was when Brian's ma would wake up and go to crying. I felt sorry for her but I wished sometimes that she would shut up. I was worried that the savages might hear her crying or that her crying and taking on would keep us from hearing the savages.

Traveling steady and easy, it took us ten days to reach Raccoon Springs. Raccoon springs was a pleasant stop and pa let us stay there for three hours. The water was fresh and cool and there was plenty of shade. It was just the kind of place to relax and rest. I learned later that more than one party of travelers had been ambushed there. Moses and Lige reported to pa after they returned from a scout and we moved two or three miles to another camping site.

Nobody complained at having to leave the cool water and shade. Everyone just fell in and we followed Lige. As unfortunate as Brian getting copperhead bit and dying was, there was some good come out of it. Pa didn't have to remind people to be 'steady' near as much.

11

The McNitt Massacre

That night, we camped in a beautiful spot not far from the Little Laurel River. We got there when the cool of the evening was just beginning to set in. It felt good after traveling and watching for both Indians and copperheads all day. I never figured out which worse, the Indians or the copperheads.

The first thing pa did was to send me and Bear out to scout the area. He sent others too but I think it was me and Bear he trusted most, especially Bear. Pa was never a man to just think that things were safe. He had to have things checked out. After me and Bear got through and the other scouts came in, pa and Bear went out again. Pa was a cautious man. Some of the men in the party complained about pa's caution and the extra work and lost sleep it cost them. None of them bucked pa on it though.

Caution was a real good thing to have on the Boone's Trace. Just taking it for granted that things were safe could get a man killed in a hurry. Whether sitting on a rock or downed tree without checking for copperheads or taking it for granted that there were no

Indians about could either one get a man dead in a hurry. Pa didn't aim to get dead in a hurry.

The point of the story I'm about to tell is that from 1775 until Kentucky was made a state, there were no safe times, The McNitt Massacre happened six or maybe four years after we camped at that beautiful place. The Boone Trace was dangerous.

I have no idea how many thousands of settlers traveled across the Boone's Trace through Cumberland Gap and into Kentucky. It was a high number and I am proud to be one of the people who came through Cumberland Gap and up the Boone's Trace. A lot of people died making the move into Kentucky. I don't know how many and I'm not sure that anyone knows for sure. When Daniel Boone first attempted to bring settlers into Kentucky, his oldest son James was tortured and killed by a group of worthless redskins. I do not believe that the exact location of his grave is known. As I said, I don't know how many settlers were killed by Indians on the trace but it could be hundreds. Most of the folks that were killed were buried close to where they died in an unmarked grave close to the Boone's Trace. Some were killed for what few possessions and some were killed by Savage worthless Indians being paid by the British to kill settlers. The attacks by hostile savage Indians were so frequent and numerous that man named William Whitley made it his mission to track down and punish the murdering savages. Whitley knew, just like I know, that there was a strong British push behind the attacks. Like me, William Whitley hated the British. I have been told that he hated them so much that when he built a race course, he deliberately raced horses opposite the direction raced in England.

That makes sense to me. Like I said, I got no use for the British or for Indians.

Like I was saying, a lot of people died on the Boone's Trace. The graves were usually hidden so the savages couldn't dig the graves up and disturb the dead. I know of only a few isolated grave spots.

Despite the large number of casualties, recognized and remembered burial spots are few. The only one I am aware of is near the spot we were camped near the Little Laurel River. It is the burial spot of the casualties of the McNitt Massacre. This place, I understand that now they call it the "Defeated Camp," is the place where a passel of settlers were attacked in September or October in either 1784 or 1785, or maybe it was in1786. This was several years after we camped at that beautiful spot.

The story goes that in the summer of either 1784 or 85 or maybe it was1786,   James McNitt -- the youngest son of a large family of Pennsylvania pioneers Robert McNitt and his wife named Catherine -- sold his homestead, which he called "Misnomer," left his fiddle in the care of his brother John, and headed down the Cumberland and Shenandoah Valleys in search of a better future. The McNitt family, I have been told, claims that he was an able and experienced adventurer, a frontiersman and Indian scout who had spent a lot of time in Kentucky.

The truth is, if all the men whose families claimed they were strong, rugged adventurous Indian scouts and experienced frontiersmen were that, we would never have heard of Daniel Boone and Simon Kenton. Sometimes a man could get that reputation and never go more than tem miles from home.
Anyway, this McNitt was named to lead them by a group of about sixty settlers, men, women and children originally from Rockbridge and Botetourt Counties, Virginia, with possibly a few folks from North Carolina. They set out later than was common for settlers. Some folks claim that they didn't leave until after harvest. I figure that it was more likely that they delayed because they wanted to sell or trade what they could not take with them for wilderness necessities. They set out on the Boone Trace. Like many other people, they were hoping for a better future west of the mountains in Kentucky.

I am not sure why they selected James McNitt to be their leader. McNitt's kinfolk have claimed that he had been scouting and adventuring among the new settlements and the Indians. If he had, I hadn't heard of it. But then again, I aint heard of everything. Whatever the reason, McNitt was selected to be the leader and the party known as the McNitt Company was attacked, many were killed and were buried at the spot now known as Defeated Camp.

The McNitt Company knew or should have known that the path they chose was dangerous. The Boone's Trace was close to The Warriors Path. Sometimes the Boone's Trace and the Warriors path overlapped. If they didn't know this, they should have got a leader who did know it. The Warrior's Path was a path used by several Indian tribes for many years. The path was used for both trading and raiding as well as for travel and hunting.

Just under two years earlier than the McNitt Massacre, on October 3, 1784, another smaller party had been murdered and mutilated on the Boone's Trace in what was known as the Moore Massacre. Two weeks earlier, a party was attacked near the spot McNitt camping spot and several McClure children were killed while their mother and an infant were captured. The captives were rescued by the efforts of William Whitley and his militia. Whenever he could, Whitley was quick and relentless about avenging Indian attacks on travelers and settlers.

Some folks claimed that the McNitt Company had traveled with caution, scouting the trail and posting sentries at night. How they knew this I don't know but that is what they claim. It is certainly possible that they did these things but if they didn't, they definitely weren't the first party to place too much trust in luck. They may have counted on the size of their party to discourage attack.

Travel in September and October was probably pleasant. A cooler climate than the heat of July and the dog days of August but with lower creeks and rivers to cross than if they had started in April or May. Even with these advantages, the terrain remained a challenge. The trace, trail or road was fairly well marked but evidence suggests few if any wagons had traveled over the trail. There weren't many settlers along the route to get information from or to ask for assistance.

The party had reason to feel relieved when they reached the area above the Little Laurel River. Dr. Thomas Walker has recorded that his party lost one horse due to a broken leg, two horses were bitten by copperheads, one man was lamed and a dog broke its leg. Even though a primitive trail had been established, the trail was still rough.

The worst of the trail was behind them. They had seen no hostiles. Some of the men were probably beginning to think of themselves as woodsmen equal to or better than Daniel Boone or Simon Kenton. They were camped near a spring in a wooded area (it must have seemed like an ideal camping spot) and felt they had safety in numbers. The McNitt party apparently felt they were reaching safer territory. They were closer to settlement stations and had seen no Indians. Their trek, though hard and tiring, had been undisturbed by hostiles. The men had lived through the years of the American Revolution, traveled through Cumberland Gap and arrived in a pleasant spot that seemed to be out of the wilderness. Overconfidence in their experience and the supposed formidability of their size eclipsed caution and caused the party to relax their defensive posture. The Promised Land was in sight. Days of vigilance without disturbance, a new life just a few days away and the natural resistance of people living on the edge of the frontier to discipline resulted in the utter relaxation of caution.

While the settlers from east of the mountains were under the impression that the war with England was ended, residents west of the mountains knew the agents of the British were still trying to stir up trouble between the white settlers and the Indians. The British have never been worth a damn. Even though Andy Jackson beat hell out of them at N 'Orleans, I still got no use for them. Savage raids and attacks on stations and travelers left no settler with any doubt that the British were still paying the Indians to attack settlers. Raids and other savage attacks would continue until General Anthony Wayne defeated them at the Battle of Fallen Timbers and chased them to the closed gates of a British fort.

It was not easy leading a party of settlers. Some people could only be led as long as they allowed themselves to be led. It is possible that McNitt was only a leader as long as he went along with the general idea of what the party wanted.

Whatever the case, the McNitt party ate supper, relaxed and planned for a future many would not have. Some of the party began playing cards. Others turned in for the night. No guards were posted.

The autumn moon shone through branches already partly bare of leaves leaving the party of 60 men, women and children in plain sight to the savage, renegade Chickamauga Indians that began to surround them. It is quite possible that the settlers' own conversation prevented them from hearing the rustle of fallen leaves as the hostile savages got in position. No one has ever mentioned if alcohol being used to lubricate the playing cards but this could help account for the party being caught unawares. Then the savage Indians attacked.

Without any mercy, the Chickamauga fell upon the relaxed camp. They killed and scalped men, women and children. Some members of the party escaped and there is no record of any live captives being taken. The livestock were stolen along with the party's baggage. Property that was not taken was ruined. Feather ticks and pillows were sliced open and feathers were strewn over the bloody camp site.

It is believed that at least 24 of the party were killed. At least 21 were killed almost immediately where they lay or sat and that others were killed trying to escape. Some folks claim that a pregnant woman hid in a hollow tree and gave birth before morning.

These same folks claim that both mother and baby survived. Folks say that a man who survived grieved for years because his young son begged him not to take him into the wilderness because he feared that the Indians would kill him.

If I remember right, in 1790 a Methodist preacher claimed, *"I saw the graves of the slain – twenty-four in one camp. I learned that they had set no guard and that they were up late playing cards. A poor woman of the company had dreamed three times that the Indians had surprise and killed them all; she urged her husband to entreat the people to set a guard but they only abused him and cursed him for his pains."*

I don't know what happened to McNitt or any of the survivors.

Of course, we didn't get ambushed like the McNitt party. I heard a low growl start from Bear and started to check when pa came up and motioned me to stay down. I saw him leave camp one way and Lige leave by another way. They were gone about an hour. When they returned, pa woke up the rest of the men and they set up a defense. It was a quiet night and the women and children were roused just shy of daybreak.

I took bear and did a scout around the camp. We found two dead Indians. Both were fresh killed. One by a knife and the other by a thrown tomahawk. I never did get told what happened.

I do know this. My pa had every camp scouted and had guards on duty every night. And I know that he checked the guard two or three times each night. That might have something to do with our party not being attacked on the Boone's Trace.

Indians attacking a small farm. Photo by Jim Cummings.

12

REDSKINS AND REDCOATS

Not all leaders were like McNitt. There was one man that I believe every Kentuckian owes more than he can afford to pay. Hell, make that every man in the United States. The man who saved the land west of the Alleghany Mountains for the United States was George Rogers Clark.

The British, during the Revolution, turned the Indians out against the Americans. The Lieutenant Governor of Canada, Lt. Colonel Henry Hamilton had spread the word among the savages that he would pay for all the scalps and captives they brought him. This shameless effort to bring attacks on innocent settlers caused him to be known as *"the Hair Buyer"*. Meanwhile, the lying British passed on to the French living in the villages on the Mississippi River in the villages of Cahokia, Bellefontaine, and Kaskaskia that wild frontiersmen from Kentucky would attack them without mercy. These villages, and Vincennes had sided with the British. The Spanish village of St. Louis had heard the same lies but did not side with the lying British. I guess the Spanish were holding their cards to see whether Spain would keep out of it or side with the Americans.

George Rogers Clark rightly figured that capturing the French settlements would put a stop to the Indian raids on the scale that Kentucky had to put up with during the *year of the bloody sevens.* Not only that, he rightly allowed that opening the Mississippi river would allow Allies and neutral nations to send the Americans war supplies through Spanish New Orleans.

Clark, was a Lieutenant Colonel in the Virginia militia. By that authority, he sent two scouts to check out the fortifications and the spirit of the people. They reported back on the weakness of the forts and the fear the people had of the Kentucky *long knives.* Clark and one other feller went back to Virginia. When they got to Martin's Station, the tale as I heard it is that nobody was there when they arrived. He arrived at Richmond and talked Patrick Henry, Virginia's governor into backing his plan. He also talked Thomas Jefferson, George Mason and Richard Henry Lee into backing his plan.

In June 1778, Clark led about 200 men on a highly secret trip down the Ohio River from Pittsburg and marching overland to Kaskaskia. The local French militia were caught completely by surprise. The fort, the village and all the people were captured without a shot being fired. The French militia commander, Chevalier Phillippe de Rocheblave, was expecting a massacre from the feared *long knives* from Kentucky. When he and the village leaders were told that there was an alliance with France that had been signed and that France had declared war against the lying British, they welcomed Clark and his small force.

Now Clark had nerve, brains and confidence. Somehow, he got the French to do most of his work for him. He got a French preacher, they called him a priest, to take a handful of Clark's men to Fort Sackville at Vincennes. This French preacher got there and told the folks about the treaty between the United States and France. After the folks found out, nothing would do but for them to hold a ceremony (the French was awful high on ceremonies) and swear to side with the Americans. A few men stayed at Fort

Sackville, more to remind the people that they were our friends than anything else. Clark then sent a handful of his militia with some local Frenchmen to Prairie du Roche and Cahokia. As soon as the folks there were told by the Frenchies that France and America were siding together, of course there had to be ceremonies to swear to back Clark and America against the British. I told you the Frenchies love ceremony.

Now it wasn't long before the British at Detroit learned what Clark had done. *Hair Buyer* Hamilton got up a force of nearly five hundred soldiers and Indians and headed for Vincennes to take back Fort Sackville. He got there sometime in December and found that the fort was defended by Captain Leonard Helm and three of Clark's force. Helm, not being foolish enough to test the five hundred against four odds, surrendered.

Right then, Clark was in a pickle. Low life savage Indians that sided with the bloody British were all around. He was low on supplies and was having to buy all his supplies on credit. He was confident that Virginia would take care of the debts but that's another story. If supplies had not been supplied by the Spanish in N' Orleans on credit, Clark would not have had supplies. Without these supplies Clark would have been forced to return to Virginia. If Clark had returned to Virginia, the northwest might have been lost to the British.

Hair Buyer Hamilton figured he would be safe until spring and let his bloody savages and militia leave. This would have normally been a good idea if he was dealing with normal men because this way he didn't have to feed his Canadians and savages. This left him with about fifty men.

The trouble for *Hair Buyer* was the force with Clark wasn't made up of normal men. These men were half hoss and half alligator that didn't know stop, back-up or quit. Their leader, George Rogers Clark, made these tough men look like they were still attached to a tit.

In late January, Clark learned that *Hair Buyer* had captured Fort Sackville. Clark knew that as soon as spring arrived, *Hair Buyer* would be coming after him. Clark could have stayed where he was and waited for the *Hair Buyer*. Clark could have returned to the Kentucky settlements and defended them. Instead, Clark decided to attack *Hair Buyer* Hamilton at Vincennes.

Clark sent his brother John with a row galley. The galley was loaded with supplies, ammunition and a swivel gun. Their job was to prevent the British from escaping by water and carry supplies that Clark's force would need.

Clark and less than 200 men, half of them local Frenchmen started to Vincennes. Vincennes was almost two hundred miles away. I have talked with men who were with Clark and believe me, they had it rough. Heavy rains had made the trails mud and made lowlands into shallow lakes. The streams were flowing over their banks from the rains. After the first couple of days, the ground was covered with water than came up over their footgear. When they got to the junction of the two branches of the Little Wabash, there were not two branches. The flood waters were so high that it was turned into a wide lake. They had to spend two or three days building a boat to carry the men and supplies across to the other bank.

When they got to the Embarrass River, they were indeed embarrassed because they could not cross. They had to go down the Embarrass to the Wabash where it took them two more days to build boats to cross the river. The men were hungry and tired. There was no game because the animals left the flood for higher ground. Clark wouldn't build fires because he didn't want his force of men to be discovered. Everybody was cold and wet.

When they got close to Vincennes, they captured five hunters on the river. The hunters told them that no, the British didn't know Clark was on his way. The hunters also said that the French at Vincennes still favored the Americans because they had been treated badly by the *Hair Buyer.*

The next day, they crossed the Wabash and had to walk in water shoulder deep for the rest of the day. They reached high ground, rested and tried to dry their clothes and gear. A day later, wet, hungry and tired they spent the night about five miles from Vincennes. The men I talked to claimed that was the coldest night of the trip and again, no fires.

The next day they were hungrier, tireder and felt both colder and wetter. They captured some Indians cooking a quarter of a buffalo. They ate the Buffalo. They spent the rest of the day eating, drying clothes and gear and waiting for dark. While camped, they captured another French hunter. He told Clark how the fort was manned and defended. Clark knew he had to strike before anyone knew how weak his force was and before the *Hair Buyer* got reinforcements.

When Clark got going, he got going quick. By force of will and confidence, he moved his small force. First off, he sent word the folks in the village that he was going to attack the fort that night and that he had a thousand men. He also sent word that they were free to keep out of the fighting if they wished. Whatever he told them must have worked because they didn't warn *Hair Buyer.*

Just before sundown, Clark assembled his force. They marched into the village with drums beating and flags flying. Clark marched them just out of sight and hurried a bunch of them back then scrambled a group back behind the last rank. Clark kept this going until he gave the fort the impression that he had over a thousand men. Clark was careful not to let the folks in the village see more than a part of his force at any one time. Clark put his men up on high ground and sent about a dozen to hide close to the fort and be ready to fire at anything that moved. The rest of the force stayed in the village and ate hot food provided by the people. They ate good too because the villagers thought they were feeding a thousand men instead of a little shy of two hundred men.

Inside the fort, *Hair Buyer* and some of his officers were just starting a game of cards. They heard a volley of shots but just thought it was some savages coming in to sell scalps. Hair Buyer just kept on dealing cards until it was reported to him that some of his men were wounded. A British doctor was allowed to escape the village into the fort. He told *Hair Buyer* that between five hundred and a thousand men surrounded the fort. Soon almost all of Clark's force of less than 200 men were shooting at anything that moved in front of a hole in the stockade.

By daybreak, the British sharply increased their firing. Clark sent one of his French captains to the fort with a demand that *Hair Buyer* surrender. He warned *Hair Buyer* that if he didn't not surrender, there would be "severe consequences." *Hair Buyer* refused and the firing continued. *Hair Buyer* tried to talk Clark out of his demand of an unconditional surrender. That was when Clark's men captured eight of *Hair Buyer's* Ottawa and Delaware Indians.

Clark paraded the captive Indians in front of the fort. He made them sit in a circle with their hands tied. Clark ordered the Indians, all of them toting settler scalps, tomahawked in front of the fort. *Hair Buyer* was afraid that if he did not surrender to what he believed was Clark's superior force, that he and all of his men would be tomahawked like the red devils Clark had ordered killed. He gave a list of surrender terms to Clark. Clark again demanded unconditional surrender and told him that cannons would soon arrive. They dickered a little while and Clark gave in on a few small things. *Hair Buyer* thought he was doing as well as any man could and surrendered.

The next morning, *Hair Buyer* and his men marched out of the fort and surrendered. Clark led his few ragged and rough men into the fort and raised the American flag. *Hair Buyer* broke down and cried when he learned that Clark did not have as large a force as he had believed.

Like I said, I have talked with a bunch of the men who were with Clark. To a man, they said that no one but Clark could have led them to victory. One thing is for dern sure. After Clark captured the *Hair Buyer,* Indian attacks slowed down for a spell.

INDIAN TROUBLE. PHOTOGRAPH BY JIM CUMMINGS

13

BRYANTS STATION

If there was any doubt as to the wickedness of the British and their savage hirelings, that doubt was put to rest in 1780. Even as we made our way from North Carolina and up the Boone Trace, the cussed redcoats and their savages were on the attack. And they brought cannon. They brought cannons and savages against settlers who were just trying to live. Men women and children were attacked by the redcoats and savage redskins.

I always figured that the reason for the wickedness of the British was that they aimed to keep Americans east of the mountains. The British officers, during the French and Indian War, saw the vastness of our country for the first time. They realized that if the settlers got over the mountains, England would be sucking the hind tit. I figure that was the reason they tried to stop westward movement in 1763. The British have always been selfish, and lower than a snake's belly.

The men, women and children in Kentucky were attacked by Captain Henry Bird, of the Eighth Regiment of his Majesty's low-life forces, and over a fifteen hundred British regulars, Canadian volunteers, Indians and Tories. They brought cannon with them and blood thirsty savages with them. His force included the renegades, Simon Girty and his brothers James and George. Captain Bird and his heathen captured about 500 men, women and children. He would have captured more but the heathen savages murdered some who tried to surrender. He forced the captives to carry goods from their own cabins over 600 miles to Detroit. When they got to Detroit, the kidnapped people were divided up among the savages and held as slaves. They were then scattered all over Canada in various Indian towns. Families were separated and most were held captive until Lige and me and General Anthony Wayne beat hell out of the Indians at the battle of fallen timbers, over ten years later.

The attack on Kentucky was, like I said, to stop America east of the Alleghany Mountains. I am glad we beat hell out of those sons of bitches. Their officer, Captain Byrd, brought the British flag and cannons into Kentucky. Bird demanded the forts at Martin's and Ruddle's stations 'surrender in the name of King George.'

Ruddle's Station was a small settlement along the South Licking River. In June 1780, Captain Byrd attacked Ruddle's Station. Byrd commenced the attack and used cannon to force the fort to surrender. The lying Captain Bird promised John Ruddle, the settlement's leader and founder an honorable surrender. He promised that everybody would be spared. This was a damn lie. When the fort gates were opened, the murdering savages forced their way in and murdered over two hundred men, women and children. Bird claimed that he didn't mean for it to happen but I got no reason to believe anything a lying British officer says.

Two days later, Bird and his cannon forced martin's Station to surrender. At Martin's Station, they took over one hundred captives. Bird claimed that he ended his campaign because he was bad upset by his savages murdering folks at Ruddle's Station. I always figured it was because the alarm was out and that the settlers were ready to attack him where his cannon couldn't be used. After all, the British knew that George Rogers was out there somewhere and he was a man to be feared.

The next station that would have been attacked was Bryant's Station.

Bryant's (or Bryan's) Station was started by four Bryant (or Bryan) brothers from North Carolina. These brothers; William, Morgan, James and Joseph were known in North Carolina by pa and Lige. William was married to a sister of Daniel Boone. Daniel Boone was married to Rebecca Bryant. A man who was right in amongst them was Will Grant. Will Grant was married to another sister of Daniel Boone. All five of these men were older woodsmen with large families. Their children were near grown and could be relied on to provide extra guns in case of an Indian attack. On their way from the Yadkin Valley to Kentucky, they were joined by two hunters. These hunters from Virginia, Cave Johnson and Will Tomlinson continued the journey with them and helped build the station. They, like us, passed over the Boone Trace and through Boonesborough.

When we passed through Boonesborough, We knew we wouldn't be staying there long. After leaving the camp close to the Little Laurel River (where a few years later a group of settlers would become part of the tale of the Boone Trace when they were defeated and twenty-four were buried in the McNitt massacre) we continued north to the Hazel Patch. At the Hazel Patch, there was a split. Boone's Trace continued north to Boonesborough and Skaggs' Trace split off to the west toward the Crab Orchard and the settlements of Logan's Fort, Fort Harrod and St. Asaphs. Boonesborough was a good place to stop because it allowed us a little more rest when other settlers were handy to take on some of the guard duty. It wasn't as bad as the year of bloody sevens but it was not a peaceful stroll either.

When we arrived at Bryant Station (some folks called it

Bryan Station and I've heard it called both so much that I don't know which one is right), settlers had only been in Kentucky for five or six years. I disremember the right number but it hadn't been long. Several small stations had been built early but after the worthless, hell-bound, bloody, British hired the Indians to attack the Kentucky settlements in 1777; the number fell off a right smart. That is why the settlers called 1777 the 'year of the bloody sevens.' If I aint bad wrong, the only places left in Kentucky were Boonesborough, Fort Harrod, and Logan's Fort.

The area around Bryant Station had been explored by early longhunters and folks looking for land. I reckon that everyone who saw the land wanted to stay on it. Now both North Carolina and Virginia are Beautiful places. I reckon the case could be made that all the states east of the Appalachian Mountains are Beautiful. They may be Beautiful but I reckon Kentucky is a sight more beautiful. I don't know why but it sure is more beautiful. Maybe it's because Kentucky is west of the Appalachian Mountains.

In 1772 or 1773, some hunters by the name of McAfee killed an elk. None of the hunters had ever seen a finer elk than that one. It was not practical to tote the elk's antlers with them but they cut them off anyway. They then tied the elk antlers to a tree on the bank of the creek it had been drinking from when it was shot. From the minute those antlers were fastened to that tree on the creek bank until this very minute; that creek has been called Elkhorn.

In 1775 some settlers were camped beside that creek while looking to claim land and start a settlement. In honor of the colonists that were murdered by the bloody British at Lexington, Massachusetts; they decided right then to name the new settlement Lexington. The settlement of Lexington was about five miles south of Bryant Station. Neither of these settlements would have mattered but pa and Lige had friends from North Carolina that settled in that area.

There were settlers from both Virginia and North Carolina in the Lexington and Bryant Station area. Early explorers and settlers such as John Floyd, James Dogglns and Hancock Taylor, William Bryan, a hunter from that section of North Carolina now known as Rowan county, and John Ellis, a Virginia French and Indian War Veteran were in the area since 1775.

These men, and other settlers like my pa and Lige and the rest of our party, could look at the beautiful fertile Kentucky lands and see a future of plenty for themselves and their families. Most people, like my pa and Lige, could see plenty of British and Indian trouble ahead. Kentucky settlers back then had to tote a rifle or musket pretty much all of the time.

Because of the danger, Kentucky land was not cheap. We paid for it with our sweat and with our blood. The Indians were paid by the bloody, worthless, British to kill or capture us. I heard from good authority that Henry Hamilton, the Lieutenant Governor up in Detroit, had a mattress that was stuffed with settlers' scalps the British had bought from the Indians. Of course, in 1780, Henry Hamilton was our captive. George Rogers Clark had captured him and the fort at Vincennes. I think they called it Fort Sackville.

As far as I'm concerned, George Rogers is as brave and good a soldier as any was in the Continental Army. I know that more lies have been told about him that than there are British and Indians in hell, but he saved Kentucky. Hell, he saved the whole Northwest Territory. Anybody wants to bad mouth George Rogers Clark in front of me had better want to fight.

Now it was told on George Rogers Clark that when he had Fort Sackville surrounded, Indian warriors showed up to sell scalps. Clark and his men captured the Shawnee and tied them up in front of the fort. Clark then demanded that Hamilton surrender. When Hamilton refused, Clark ordered his men to tomahawk the Indian. Hamilton, believing that the fort was surrounded by superior numbers, surrendered. The story is that Hamilton was madder than a stepped on snake when he learned that he was not outnumbered. Men that was there claimed that the Hair buyer cried when he saw he had been tricked.

Because the British were hiring the Indians to fight the Kentucky settlers, homesteads and stations were built, abandoned and rebuilt when the settlers returned.

Because of the success of George Rogers Clark against the Shawnee after the cowardly Bird brought his murdering Indians down against Ruddle's and Martin's, settlers began to come again. When we had arrived, there were several empty cabins. Now there was a rush of settlement. Settlers, mostly from Virginia, made the station stronger than ever. Some of those who came after us were John Ellis, with his family and Negroes; three Craig brothers, Elijah, John and Jeremiah; Joseph Stucker and relatives, and John Martin, John Turner and a handful of Mitchells and Hendersons. The new settlers added and cabins to the station most important, increased the number of rifles to protect the station against redcoats and redskins. After Martin's and Ruddle's fell, Bryan was the most exposed settlement north of the Kentucky River.

Lexington was close by but was less vulnerable because the founders had included a spring inside the stockade. The time would come when we all wished we had that advantage.

We wintered pretty good but when spring brought warmer weather, the savages came too. We lost a few settlers who ventured out alone or who were working in their fields without a guard. Random attacks continued throughout the summer. Sometimes Lige would leave for a few days and come back to report. Once he brought back three scalps that he buried in graves of scalped settlers.

We survived. The number of settlers grew and things began to look up. The word reached us in early winter that more settlers were on the way. Each new man meant at least one new rifle for defense. Kentucky needed more strong arms and more rifles. The fact that there weren't enough rifles was brought us by the news of Estill's defeat in the spring of 1782.

James Estill, established a station approximately fifteen miles from Boonesborough. On March 19, 1782, an empty raft was seen floating down the Kentucky River past Boonesborough. The alarm was immediate. Estill immediately gathered twenty-five men from nearby stations and led them after the Indians. Most of the fort's men followed Estill, Leaving his station undermanned. On the next day twenty-five marauding savages suddenly appeared at Estill's Station and launched a surprise attack. A young girl and a slave named Monk were caught. The savages immediately killed and scalped the young girl. The savages did this in plain sight of the women who were helpless in the station. Monk kept his head however. He told the savages that there was a strong force of men inside the station. The trick worked and the savage redskins left. The fort sent two boys to find the search party and tell them about the raid. Estill and his party were looking for Indian sign on the Kentucky River. The boys found them and gave them the bad news.

Estill and his men found the trail left by the savages and went after them. They caught up with the savages at the Little Round Mountain. They surprised three savages who had stopped to skin a buffalo. The savages ran back to the main body of Indians. Firing by both sides began immediately. Both sides tried to find cover. The odds were even until a man named Miller fled the fight with six other cowards. This left Estill and his men outnumbered.

The battle didn't last long. After Miller fled, the savages realized that they outnumbered the settlers. Taking advantage of this, they rushed across the creek and attacked Estill's force in hand-to hand combat with knives and tomahawks. Several of Estill's men were killed in the charge. Captain Estill, who already had a broken arm, was wounded again. Estill was unable to fight off a stronger adversary with his broken arm and was mortally wounded.

A settler named Proctor immediately killed the savage. Will Irvine was wounded in the battle. Joseph Proctor helped him mount Estill's horse and ride to safety. Proctor, at great risk found and escorted Irvine to Bryan's Station, twenty miles away.

A group of fifty settlers returned to the battle site to bury the dead. Only a handful of Estill's men survived, not counting Miller and the cowards who left with him. They don't count anyway.

In April, about two weeks after Estill's defeat, Virginians arrived from Gilbert's Creek, providing welcome reinforcements Bryant's and other settlements.

I was at Bryant's Station when some newcomers were being welcomed. There were three men without families. All of the men looked a little familiar. You know how it is when there is something you recognize but you just can't pin down what it is and you don't feel sure enough to ask, that's how I felt. One of the men glanced at me and was suddenly as still as a rock. I figured he had recognized me and would come over to say howdy. He didn't. He said something to the other two and they began to stroll away from the cabins. It was when they walked into the shade that it come to me that I had seen these three men walk away before. I would have sworn it was Jason Smith and the two men who tried to lure my pa out of the cabin the night the Tories tried to trick pa into coming out of our cabin in the Yadkin valley in North Carolina. I was convinced but without seeing all their faces, I couldn't be sure.

That night, I told pa. Pa puffed on his pipe a spell and said, As long as they don't bother us, we'll let them be. There's enough fighting to do with the Indians without borrowing trouble with white men."

That is what pa said but I took notice that pa checked the fling and priming on every gun we had in the cabin.

Like everything else, I have heard a lot of tales about forting up. I know some folks claim we all lived inside a fort. Now that just aint so, however, a week forting up might seem like a month or so.

First place, most of the forts weren't proper forts. They weren't called even forts. They were called stations. A station was a cabin or several cabins within a stockade. The walls of the cabins formed part of the stockade walls. The roofs sloped steeply inward so that a burning arrow could be swept off before it had a chance to catch the roof afire. Some of the larger stockade areas could cover two acres, which was good if you had enough rifles to defend two acres of walls. Most stations were smaller. As far as I know, all stockades had four walls. No pioneer station had any cannon.

I heard that Matildy Craig claims that folks got to be real close and friendly after they forted up for a spell. Yep, we got close. So close that we bumped into each other. If the weather was rainy or cold, there might be six or eight families in one cabin. If the nights weren't too wet or cold and had a comfortable breeze, most people slept outside. That way you weren't as apt to get stepped on while sleeping. After a week in a station, folks began to tire of their neighbors. After a month, you might be ready to join the attackers.

The truth is, no one wanted to stay forted up any more than they had to stay forted up. None of us would have if it wasn't necessary.

The women quarreled the most. Men knew that if they quarreled, they would have to fight and fighting could get someone bad hurt. The women could argue and quarrel without it coming to a fight. In fact, when push come to shove, frontier women were awful handy to have around.

Some forts had springs inside the fort or real close. Every fort should have had a water supply inside the fort but most didn't. Pa had mentioned that Bryant's Station should have a well dug but nobody seemed to want to be part of the effort.

The stockade walls, that weren't part of the cabin walls, were made from trees chopped down from nearby and set together in a ditch or trench. The walls were usually between nine and twelve feet high and pointed at the end sticking up. These logs, when pushed or jammed together, could stop arrows and rifle or musket fire. Unfortunately, as Ruddle's Station showed, they could not stand up to cannon fire.

I have heard people tell that each station had a blockhouse at each corner. Well some did and some didn't. Some stations were lucky if they had two angled across from each other. These blockhouses hung over the outside walls about two foot and were handy for fetching an Indian next to the wall and under the firing holes in the stockade walls.

The log cabins that formed part of the stockade walls had shingled roofs that were steep to allow fire arrows to skitter off without setting the roof afire. There were no cabin doors on the side of the cabin that was part of the stockade walls. Doors and shutters had leather hinges. Some of the windows might be covered with oiled paper, some did not have any cover.

The people inside these stations got to know each other too well. It didn't do to have a falling out with your husband or wife because everybody knew all about it in a hurry. On a hot day, nobody had to ask where the necessary was because you could smell it all over the stockade. Yep, a week forted up in a stockade could seem like a month or two. Maybe longer.

Forting could be tiresome, tedious and sometimes dangerous. Photograph by Jim Cummings, graphicenterprises.net

14

ATTACK AT BRYANT'S STATION

Bryan's Station was growing in the summer of 1782. It had over forty cabins inside a stockade settlement or station. A blockhouse at each corner provided an overlook of the surroundings and the pointed stockade pickets were over ten feet high.

Several cabins were outside the stockade. Other buildings such as smoke houses, sheds and animal pens. A garden full of vegetables and over one hundred acres of corn were outside the stockade.

In hindsight, we weren't as ready as we should have been. We all knew that George Washington had forced Cornwallis to surrender the past October at Yorktown, over in Virginia. A lot of people hoped that meant the bloody British and bloody savages would leave us alone. Lige didn't think so. I didn't think so. Pa damn sure didn't think so. But, as a settlement, we hadn't done enough to prepare for an Indian attack. One thing that pa tried to push for but didn't get done, was digging a well inside the stockade. We didn't have enough scouting parties out looking for the red dogs. A few men, like Lige, spent a lot of time scouting. A few men but not enough.

Lige was the first to bring us warning that redcoats and

redskins were crossing the Ohio River. Shortly afterwards, a rider on a sweated horse told us that some settlers had met the Indians at the Upper Blue Licks and had been defeated by overwhelming numbers. At that moment, there were less than fifty rifles inside the stockade. He added that he figured this might be the same bunch who had captured children down at Hoy's Station but that he couldn't be sure. Everyone was demanding that every man turn out to chase down these savage rascals and teach them a lesson.

The general feeling was that the red dogs Lige had seen crossing the Ohio River were the same that had attacked Hoy's Station and bested the force on the Upper blue Licks. There was a big uproar to defeat these red devils with a bigger force. Lige and Pa weren't convinced.

Pa decided that we could work our farm during the day and sleep inside the stockade at night. He hung a canvas we could sleep under even if it rained.

Fortunately, cooler tempered men saw that we needed to keep enough men at each station to protect the stations. It was a good thing we did, because the hellhounds were on their way. We never knew for sure how many were sent against us. Boone always said that the Indians alone numbered over four hundred and we figured there to be over one hundred British. This didn't count the renegades the Girty's brought with them. We never did find out what the exact strength of the invading force was and probably never will.

The enemy was confident in their strength and traveling light. The redcoats and redskins figured they would take care of business quick. They figured to make short work of the most exposed settlements and finish by driving all settlers east of the mountains. The British and their savage dogs figured they could live off what they stole from the settlers. The British have always been pretty lowlife that way.

The Shawnee had canoed down the Little Miami River. Full of confidence that their strength would outnumber the settlers and not having to be weighed down by baggage of any kind, they were eager to let loose their devilishness. They crossed the Ohio River, where part of their party was spied by Lige. They moved quickly down the Licking River and arrived at Bryant's station during the night of August 15nth. When they got to Bryant's station, they surrounded the stockade and settled in to wait for the settlers to expose themselves. As far as the savages could tell, there had not been a single word of warning to alarm the settlers.

It appeared that Girty and the British had led their savage dogs to an easy victory over sleeping settlers. But they reckoned without another savage dog. Bear's low throated growls woke me up and I woke. Pa. Pa woke Lige the rest of the family. Girty and his savage dogs had reached the heart of Kentucky without being seen but Bear knew they were there. Girty probably felt pretty pleased with himself. His whole force took positions under the cover of the creek bank or the brush near the bank. They crawled as close to the fort as they could get.

The savages could be easily and completely hidden by the tall, lush plentiful brush. If the brush had not been there, they could have still concealed themselves in the acres of tall corn. In fact, some of them were posted inside the trees and acres of corn. The main part of the force was hidden in the canebrake and full grown brush that were beside the spring we all got our water from.

Captain Caldwell, Girty and the Indian leaders weren't sure about how many men with rifles were inside the stockade.

The enemy was confident in their strength and traveling They doubtlessly hoped that most of the men had volunteered to go help the party that had been bested at the Upper Blue Licks but they could not be sure.

Now I always figured the redcoats and redskins had made a big mistake by trying to lure a rescue party away from the settlements. The same reasons that caused a rescue party to be formed caused settlers to fort up inside the stockades. A lot of settlers figured the war was winding down after General George Washington whipped Cornwallis and a lot of people had let their guard down. A lightning raid that caught settlers outside the stockades might have been successful and might have forced us to either be killed, captured or to flee east from Kentucky.

Caldwell, Girty and the redskins decided to send out a scout and try to capture someone who could tell them what was going on inside the stockade. Their figuring was that if they couldn't capture someone, they could raise a little fuss and cause the stockade to react in a way that exposed its strength or weakness.

Of course, the hell hounds hid outside the stockade had reckoned without the wariness of Bear. Enough people were already alerted to calm the people inside the walls and prevent them from panicking. The British plan might have worked if cooler headed men like pa hadn't insisted enough men be kept in the station to protect the station.

Neither Caldwell nor Girty knew that we had any idea what their real strength was. Well, we didn't really know how many there were, but we knew it was not a group of five or six stragglers. We knew the total number was closer to five hundred or even six hundred hiding out around the stockade walls.

When the settlers inside the stockade did not react like they were surrounded by an army. Caldwell and Girty grew more convinced that their army had not been discovered and that they still held the high card of surprise. They did not know that their high card had been trumped by a savage dog named Bear.

Caldwell and Girty held their supposed surprise card close and waited for their chance to play it. While they held that card close, the settlers played their cards close. Everyone went out of their way to show no alarm and act as normal as they could. Normally, a large force against a station would cause a force to arrive from other stations to help them out. Caldwell hoped this would happen as he wanted to ambush the rescue force. The redcoats and redskins have used this trick several times before and since the attack at Bryant's station. This time, however, there was no visible alarm. There was absolutely no sign given to those outside the walls that we had any idea a major attack was about to take place.

Under pa's directions, the settlers began to prepare for the attack we knew would come shortly. Pa told them that since the Indians had tried to trick us, that we should turn the tables and trick them instead.

Tom Bell and Nick Tomlinson immediately departed the stockade. Their job was to ride to Lexington and warn the folks there what was going on. They got away without any hindrance, probably because Caldwell and Girty wanted to draw the rescuers into a fatal ambush. In order to complete the deception that we were not aware of the enemy presence, the livestock were loosened to return to their regular daytime range. The red devils had to keep from exposing themselves or they would let us know that they were around us. We had to buy time by not letting the redcoats and redskins know that we knew they were there.

The red scouts showed themselves as though they might be stragglers from the party that had attacked Hoy's Station rather than as a part of a larger attacking force. One of the scouts was shot by Jim McBride. Now Jim always claimed to have the first kill of the siege but there was so much going on that I wouldn't swear to it. Pa and Lige had both been out armed with just knives and tomahawks. They had to clean their blades when they returned but neither was given to brag about killing redskins.

When other settlers heard the loud blast in the early dawn

of McBride's shot, they gathered guns and ammunition together and ran to the stockade. Settlers ran with children strapped to their backs. Others who had not received whispered warnings from pa and Lige made it to the fort without harm. Jim Morgan was one who made it to the stockade carrying his baby. It wasn't until he got there that he found that his wife wasn't running beside or behind him. Jim Morgan like to went crazy but the men kept him quiet to fool the Indians into believing we didn't know how bad the threat was that we faced.

Captain Caldwell, the red coat commander, is said to have admitted that the scouting party failed. He even said that not only did it fail, but that it was a failure of the leadership of the scouting party. Caldwell never did figure out how the settlers were warned. He did not have any idea as to how the folks at Bryant's station discovered that the stockade was surrounded by a large force. Caldwell probably wouldn't have known if Bear had bit him on his ass. Bear's warning put pa and Lige outside looking and listening to the savage army settling down. Simon Girty and Caldwell had come up with a good plan, but their plan wasn't as good as one good dog.

Of course, the intent of Caldwell and Girty was for most of the men to be out of the settlement on a mission to punish the savages we were already aware of in the region. This might have worked if men like my pa hadn't insisted enough men be left to protect the stations.

After the gates had been closed after Tom and Nick left for Lexington, the concern of water was brought up. Rather the concern was no water, because all water was got from the spring near the fort. We were in the hot dog days of mid-August and now it was too late to dig a well inside the stockade.

The first thing every morning, the women and girls would go to the spring and return with water for drinking and cooking. Without that water, we didn't stand a chance. The folks talked it over. It was decided that the only choice we had was to keep everything as normal as possible. That meant the women and girls, without any men noticeably guarding them, would have to go for the water. None of the men liked the idea. The only other options we could come up with were to try to hold out without water or surrender. We knew what had happened when Ruddle's and Martin's had surrendered. We knew that if the men went for water, the redcoats and redskins would know they had been discovered. The men would be attacked and the fort would fall. If the women went just like they suspected nothing was wrong, as was their regular early morning custom, the enemy might believe that they still held the element of surprise and hold off an attack to keep surprise on their side.

It was a gamble. It was a gamble that could have gone either way. Even if the leaders would want to hold off and try to get a better advantage, some of the Indians could act on their own and attempt to capture or kill some or all of the women. Indians were sometimes notional and not always predictable. I made myself a promise right then that if harm came to any of my kin or friends, that I would be rougher on the Indians than Lige had ever been.

The women, to their everlasting fame, did not hesitate. They did not waste time on tearful farewells or any foolishness. They gathered all of the buckets, piggins and large gourds they could carry and gathered together. There were quick hugs and a few last words. I was surprised when Lucy, Ben's sister, came over and hugged me. I didn't know what to say or do. I just hugged her back and found that I didn't want to let her go. Some of the women changed to their lightest shifts and some concealed knives under their garments. The women talked among themselves and came up with their plan.

They came up with a good plan but good plans had failed before. Part of their plan was to make their effort appear to be as routine and everyday as they possibly could. To this end, they left the fort gates laughing and gossiping. They had already decided that even if they saw an Indian, that they would pretend they hadn't. None of us, not the women going for water or the men waiting in the fort, knew if they would return or if there would be a massacre.

I don't think that any person who was there would ever forget that morning, Friday of the 16th of August, 1782. The brave and heroic pioneer women of Bryant's Station leaving the sure protection of the stockade and strolling into possible death. Their pretended cheerful banter covered the fear they all felt. The springs were out of range of most of the guns in the stockade but men were already pulling loads and replacing them with double powder charges. We were careful not to appear to be watching the women. I saw grown men wipe away tears. I looked at pa and Lige. They were both watching with their flintlocks ready and their lips were moving. I finally figured out that they were praying. I then noticed that I was praying too.

Some of the women at the springs did see Indians hiding in the cane fields and brush. They simply pretended they didn't and casually filled their buckets, piggins and gourds with water. One of the women later said that her biggest fear was that the men in the stockade would get too worried and charge out on a rescue mission that would get everybody killed. She was probably right. Waiting behind those walls was one of the hardest things we ever did but probably not as hard as going to the springs for water.

It took nearly an hour for the women to get all the buckets and gourds filled with water and walk back to the gate. It was hard, but we let them through the gate as though they had not been in danger of being massacred by the hellhounds hidden outside.

I don't think I'll ever feel as glad as I did when the women walked through the gates and into the fort. I still remember pa saying "Steady, steady now" to keep the men from showing that we knew the Indians were still there by the way they welcomed their wives and daughters and best women. As soon as they stepped to one side, the women were grabbed and hugged. When Lucy came in, she looked at me and I stepped toward her. I reached out for her and she put both arms around me like she was drowning and I was a tree. I had no idea that she had changed from a ten or twelve year old girl into a young woman until her arms were around me that day.

The water was put away and more than one person echoed pa's cautions about using it sparingly. One of the women said that it had better last because she wasn't making that trip amongst the savages again.

Even then, Caldwell and Girty thought their surprise was still safe. They waited and we waited. We knew the force from Lexington would have been warned of the large force lying in ambush. We hoped they would not approach until they had the strength to overcome the force lying in wait. Of course, we knew that we were going to hunker down and not go off chasing Indians that we knew were waiting for us.

Girty didn't know as much as we did. He kept waiting for a group from the fort to ride after the few scouts that had been seen earlier and into his ambush. That plan had and would work many times but not this time.

Shortly after the women returned from the springs, Girty got tired of waiting. Time had passed without the departure of a force to scout for the several "stragglers" that had been exposed to the settlement earlier. Girty decided to draw most of the defenders away from the northwestern side of the fort and weaken it so that a surprise attack by his main force could overwhelm it. Girty had a small group of Indians attack the opposite side of the stockade. Girty had every reason to believe that the majority of the garrison would move to stop the threat and give chase when the hostiles retreated. He figured this would leave the opposite side of the stockade defenseless and vulnerable to be overwhelmed quickly.

In this case, Girty was outsmarted by pa and the men in

the fort. Pa and Lige, during their night time scout had discovered the fort was surrounded. Pa made sure every man understood that every wall had to be defended and that no wall could ever be abandoned. Because of Bear's early warning and the scout by Pa and Lige, Girty did not have the advantage he thought he had. We knew where his forces were hiding and knew at once what evil devilishness he was up to almost before he did. We saw right away that the heathen devils wanted us to chase them. This time we did the unexpected.

While the small force attacked, yelling and shooting, we pretended confusion. The Indians were running and bellering and shooting to beat the dickens. I can still remember pa telling the men, "steady, steady now," and making sure there were men at each wall. Then he had the gates swung open.

When the gates were open where the false attack was taking place, pa and Lige and about a dozen others ran through the gates firing at the savages and yelling. They took time to aim and we saw a few Indians drop. The men hollered like they were all set to charge after the Indians.

This fooled Girty and his Indians into believing we had fallen for their trap. Pa and Lige led the men only ran far enough to draw a large volley of return fire. Pa, figuring they had done what they set out to do, turned the men and they ran back through the gates. They got back inside not one second too early. The impatient savages lying hidden in ambush heard the shooting. They took this to mean that their trick had worked. Believing that the northwest side would be unprotected and easy to take, Girty led his red devils as they charged from their hiding places toward what they believed was an undefended wall.

I still remember the sight of mostly naked, hideously painted savages charging toward the western gate. They were hollering and bellering. Some of them were carrying torches. There were more savages there than I had seen at one place in my life, up to that time. Fire was a new threat and an unexpected danger to the settlement. Fire was more feared by settlers than all the rifles and tomahawks of the savage red horde of hostiles could carry. Like I said, it was the hot dog days of summer and our cabins and stockades were tinder-dry. If fire hit the station, then the fiddles were playing and the dance had started. The savages were never far from the fort and they were getting closer in a hurry. Let me be clear, these redskins figured they already had the battle won. They were all whetted to begin massacring and looting. They wanted to take captives and rape and have a big time. They were right in step when the fiddlers changed their tune. Without warning, the supposedly empty walls of the stockade unleashed volley upon volley of rifle fire. I fired during the third volley. I left my rifle with Lucy and fired a double load of buck and ball from the Brown Bess. I knew it would spread .30 caliber balls in a wide arc against the charging savages. I hoped a lot of them would be left wounded and suffering. I don't know how many were left suffering but we sure as hell surprised the dickens out of them. Their war hollering turned to pain hollering. By the third and fourth volley, they were in a panic. The same women who had already behaved so heroically, now reloaded the fired weapons. We men took the loaded weapon and returned to line up behind a firing port.

The Indians ran every which a way. A few managed to throw torches over the wall. We shot them down like shaking apples out of a tree. Before I had a chance to get a third loaded rifle, the only Indians to be seen were the killed red devils scattered on the grassy slope around the stockade.

That was one problem taken care of but now we had another problem. The sheds outside the stockade that the torches had landed on were burning. The flames were hot and fierce and for a while we weren't sure we could stop the fire. We didn't. We didn't stop the fire, that is. What we couldn't change, God changed. Strong winds came from the east and blew the flames and sparks away from the station. The cabins that had caught were soon burned down to embers and ashes but no other buildings or the stockade were set afire by the burning cabins.

We felt pretty good about things. All of the women and girls were safe inside the fort. We had fought off an attack of savages and we weren't burned out. I felt good because Lucy had up and hugged me twice. We all felt pretty good because we were sure that the British had not brought any cannons with them. If there had been cannon, Bryant station would have fallen like Ruddle's Station and Martin's Station. As long as they didn't have any cannon, we could hold out until help got to us or until the Indians gave up.

Now remember, this was August 1782. Cornwallis had surrendered in October 1781. The peace talks had already commenced. There was absolutely no honorable reason for the bloody British to be leading an attack against settlements in Kentucky. Of course, we all know the bloody British are lower than a snake's belly and have absolutely no honor. You might even say that if it weren't for dishonor, they would have no kind of honor. I had no use for the sorry, worthless British then and I got less use for them now.

Some in the fort began to worry when we didn't see reinforcements from Lexington. We knew it would take a while for them to raise a big enough force to attack the savages that surrounded us, but it seemed to be taking longer than it should have. Some folks was worried that Tom and Nick had been captured or killed. They brought this concern to pa.

"Look at it this way," pa told the group. "If they had been killed, Girty would have dragged their bodies out to show us that we had no hope of help coming. And if they were captured, Girty would have already been bragging about it and maybe torturing them."

By the time pa was finished talking, people were convinced that Tom and Nick had got through. We later found out that they had galloped their horses flat out to Lexington. They got to Lexington to find out that most of the men had been led away to give aid to Hoy's station. It was a good thing for Lexington that Girty hadn't attacked there instead of Bryant's Station because Lexington might have been easier to take.

With all available men decoyed away from the real scene of action, more messengers had to be sent after them. The hard riding messengers caught up with the militia from Lexington at Boone's Station, which stood about ten or twelve miles north of Boonesborough. Some settlers on were already there and raring to go. Soon, armed reinforcements, were on the way to fight the redcoats and the redskins.

Back at Bryant's Station, Girty and his red hellhounds were doing what they did best. They had lost so many men when they tried to take the fort that they weren't ready to try it again. Instead, they tried to stay hid out of sight and damage as much property and crops as they could.

From hiding, the red hellhounds fired at and into the fort from all directions. Fire seemed to come from behind every rock, every stump and tree. Lead balls rained into the fort from the brush, the corn fields, and the hemp fields and from the cane. By the end of the day, we had lost two killed and one wounded. But we got in our licks too. But the sharpshooting was not all one sided.

The tale was told that little Betsy Johnson ran and told her ma, "Ma, Jacob just killed an Indian!"

Her ma is said to have replied, "That's just one Injun, there's plenty out there."

We took a lot of shots from a tall sycamore. If we saw the limbs move we got behind some cover. The tall sycamore stood on the north side of the creek.

Lige watched the tree and said, "I think I see him."

Lige fired and an Indian and his rifle came falling down the sycamore. Both Indian and rifle landed on the ground.

Pa and Lige cautioned us to save out ammunition and not to shoot until we had a clear target that was in range. So we hunkered down inside the fort and waited for something to shoot at. I don't think I fired three shots that day after we fought off the charge at the northwest wall.

The hell hounds tried to burn us out again. After several hours of gunfire that didn't really hurt the stockade or the people inside it, the savages shot flaming arrows into the fort. It was a good idea since the first attempt to burn us out came close to working. The torches that had almost worked before could only be thrown from short distances from the walls. You can bet that any hellhound that tried to get that close was going to be shot before they got within flinging distance. We had already showed Caldwell, Girty, and their savages what our gunfire could do to any hellhounds who got close. Knowing that charging with a torch was suicide, the savages resorted to flaming arrows.

Fortunately for those of us inside the stockade, many of the arrows burned out before landing. Any flaming arrows that landed on the steep inward sloping roofs skittered off the roofs before they could catch the roof shingles afire. Oh there were plenty of burning arrows. They fell on the roofs by the dozens, but none caused any problems. What few arrows that didn't skitter off were brushed off by the boys of the settlement who were posted on the roofs.

While watching some or the attackers dodging from cover to cover, one got my attention I couldn't swear to it but I thought it was Jason Smith. It was a right smart while before things calmed down enough for me to tell pa and Lige about my suspicions. When I told them, they looked at each other and just nodded. Turned out that Lige had caught a brief look and figured it was Jason Smith.

"Well, if he is killed attacking us, then we'll know," pa told us. About then the action got all hot and heavy and we didn't have time to talk about Jason Smith.

While the savage forces tried to shoot from cover, many of them were shot trying to hurl their flaming messages into the fort. I aint a bit sorry that we killed so many of them. If they hadn't hired on to fight for the bloody redcoats, they might be alive today.

We learned later that day that the hell bound renegade, Simon Girty tried to prevent reinforcements from getting to us.

Girty had not only failed to capture the stockade, he had lost a lot of redskins trying. He knew that Lexington would send men to help us and set up an ambush out of sight of those of us in the fort. He rightly figured that the armed response from Lexington would try to enter the fort by the northeastern gate, he put most of his savage hellhounds at the upper end of the trail coming from Lexington. He had them hide completely out of sight, assuring them that the two riders they had allowed to escape would return with a force they could ambush.

Girty placed his savage hellhound without interference from us because he moved them in a wide circle out of our view. He then placed them where the stockade could not provide any assistance to the rescuers. Girty had not counted on Tom and Nick having all the information that they carried. Pa and Lige had scouted the enemy pretty good and gave Tom and Nick a pretty good estimate of their strength.

When all of Girty's hellhounds were in place, all firing by the attackers stopped. There was no noise from the hidden ambushers and there were none visible. The whole area seemed to be still and waiting.

About midafternoon, the volunteers arrived within sight of Bryant's Station. The volunteers, to a man, were hot, dusty and tired. They were prepared more for a fight than for the stillness. Their leader halted them and the officers gathered to decide what to do. They could not hear or see any sign of an enemy. The only sounds they heard was the wind blowing. I heard one of the men say later that it was too quiet to be real.

The quietness made the rescuers more wary than a war cry would have. But the quiet told the experienced frontiersmen more than a war cry could have told them. The silence seemed heavy with the evil around them. The presence of the silent horde caused the very birds in the area to be quiet.

The force leaders knew that the enemy was there as though they had just stepped on a couple of the heathen. They talked and finally decided to send a small group of horsemen from Boone's Station and Lexington would make a mad dash toward the stockade. With a loud yell, the small group spurred their horses up the trail toward the stockade.

When the horsemen took off, a group of footmen dashed into the cornfield and made their way toward the stockade. When the advance was ordered, the force on foot quickly and as quietly as possible moved through the rows of tall corn.   The galloping horses of the mounted group raised a massive cloud of dust from the dog days dry ground.   Their charge created a fog of dust that did much to hide them from the redskin ambushers.
Like a tornado, the horsemen rushed up the narrow dusty trail surrounded by more than 300 savages who were suddenly yelling and firing their muskets. Most of the redskins fired without having a clear target to shoot at.   The galloping, shouting horsemen passed through a gauntlet receiving fire from both sides of the trail. The black powder smoke mixed with the dust and hid the horsemen as well as a sudden darkness could have hidden them.

The hell of gunfire and angry savages was such that I feared no rider would reach the fort alive. But they did. Every single horse and rider entered the gates of the stockade without a scratch.

Lige always said that the horses' feet raised so much dust that the savages couldn't see the horses and their riders.

I always figured it was providence as much as the dust that saved the riders. Of course the savages aint never been as smart as white men. I aint never met one as smart anyway and I have met a sight of white men that weren't real smart.

The three or four hundred redskins all firing their muskets all at once caused a big to-do along the trail and it left the savages with unloaded muskets. While they began to come out of hiding and reload their muskets, the rest of the relief militia from Lexington dodged into the corn field and real quick was out of sight. The high corn hid them pretty good and the redskins were madder 'n a bunch of hornets in a kicked nest. They were bad upset. The militia's quick move into the corn saved them. Moving into the corn and the redskins not having loaded guns, that is. The redskins were dumb of course but even a dumb redskin knows better than to charge after armed militia with unloaded muskets.

Inside the stockade, we heard the angry hollering of the redskins as they tried to get an advantage over the unseen men of the militia. The militia, either by plan or happenstance, spread out in the corn field. They ran deeper into the acres of corn and away from our stockade. Some of the men in the militia from Lexington were so old that this was the only way they could have escaped. Some ran straight down the rows of corn and depended on their speed to allow them to escape.

Some of the militia got some distance from the redskins and hunkered down. There they checked their priming and adjusted their knives and tomahawks so they were in easy reach. They knew that the redskins might find them but they figured they could take at least one or two and maybe still have a chance to get away.

The confusion helped the militia. Three redskins fired a volley at what they supposed were militia hiding in the corn. When they fired, several other redskins fired in the same general direction. They then ran, yelling and screaming, toward the spot of the movement they had shot at only to discover a dead redskin and a wounded redskin.

After that, the firing went down a great deal. The redskins tried but were never able to organize a sweep of the cornfield. When the dust settled, two of the Lexington militia were killed and four were wounded. We didn't know if any of the redskins were killed but we found the stinking corpses of killed Indians inside the cornfield for the next month.

Inside the stockade, we decided that without cannon being used against us, we could hang on as long as we needed to hang on. It was just a matter of hunkering down and keeping them out of the stockade.

The terrible chase by the savage hellhounds was easy to follow by just listening to the hollering of the redskins. We finally figured out that they were probably yelling to keep one of their own force form shooting them by mistake. We could tell where they were by the paths they made breaking down the cornstalks. It was all one big confusion of yelling, breaking and tramping down corn and the swaths cut by groups of redskins chasing the militia. Fortunately, most of the militia were already long gone by then. They had either gone across the field and hid or were running like hell ahead of the redskins. The reason that no militia had stopped to put up a fight was that they were already long gone.

It was close to sunset when the angry and frustrated red skinned savages stopped the chase of the militia from Lexington. From that minute until it was too dark to see, the ruined and wrecked everything they could. They set fire to every building outside the stockade. Cabins, sheds, corncribs, and barns were set afire by the red skinned savages. They tore down the rail fences and used the rails to cook with. They set the hemp fields afire and pulled up the vegetables. The cut down or knocked down the corn. They killed all of the settlement's livestock that they could find. They killed over 300 hogs and 150 head of cattle, the few sheep the settlers kept for the wool were killed. Every horse not inside the stockade walls was stolen. The redskin's destruction did not stop until it was too dark to continue.

Hostile Indians daring the settlers to leave the stockade and fight them, while they looted the settlers goods, livestock and crops.

The campfires were then lit and the and the savages used the fence rails to roast the best of the settlers' stock that they had killed that evening.

The Indians were not happy. They were tired and ready to leave. Most of them wondered if they were going to be able to take the stockade. The redskin leaders called a council that included Girty and Caldwell. With a council, whatever they decided would be decided without any one man having to take the blame.

The council didn't last long and no one among the

redskins thought the stockade could be taken without cannon. Nobody argued that by now, news of the attack had spread as far as Fort Harrod and Logan's Fort, as well as other smaller stations. The Indians wanted to leave right away.

Simon Girty, wanted to please his British bosses by succeeding. He pushed his way through the crowd to a high stump in a hemp field. He climbed atop the stump and hollered at the stockade.

"Ho the fort! Do you know who I am?" He paused and waited but did not get an answer.

"I am Simon Girty and I am in charge here. I have you right where I want you. I have five hundred Indians with me and another five hundred with cannon will be here tomorrow. If you surrender now, I can protect you."

Girty took a breath and continued. "If you don't surrender now, I cannot be responsible for what happens. Furthermore, the reinforcements will be bringing cannon. If you continue to resist, the cannon will destroy the stockade and I will not be able to stop the Indians from what they will do. I can
protect you and your families now, but when my Indians have hot blood and see the walls fall, I won't be able to stop them.

Now those of us inside the fort had absolutely no faith in Girty's promise to protect us. We knew what had happened at Ruddle's Station and we knew what devilish hellhounds Girty had with him. We were mad at the burning of our cabins and buildings and the killing of our stock. Many of us had already decided that when we got a chance to do the same to their villages, that we would do it. We knew that after even one more day, we would be short on water and food. We also knew we would not surrender to Girty, his red devils or to the bloody redcoats.

We remembered that Girty had been at Ruddle's Station, and what had happened there. We knew that women and children had been tortured and murdered when they were taken as "British captives" back to Ohio. We weren't going to surrender.

Pa was quietly telling us, "Steady, steady now."

Aaron Reynolds, however was not one given to staying calm. He ran up to a firing port and answered Girty.

"Hey Girty, we all know you. I have two shit eating dogs that are just like you! I call one dog Simon and I call the other dog Girty." I take a switch to them every time they need it just like I'll take a switch to you."

Aaron Reynolds, his voice full of scorn, continued, "Come to think of it, my dogs both look better than you do. Bring on your damn cannon, if you got any cannon. You're such a liar that I don't believe you. Bring on your damn cannon and be damned to you. And if you or any of your heathen get inside these walls, we will beat hell out of you with a pile of switches that we have stacked up here just to do that very thing. We won't have to. We're expecting the whole country to be here by tomorrow. If you and your murdering heathen are still here, we will have your hides and scalps drying on the tops of cabins."

None of us believed Reynolds' brags but it turned out to be the right thing to tell them. Girty claimed to be sorry that he probably would not be able to save us from the savages but the next morning, the redcoat British, Girty, and the redskins were gone. Unbelievably, thankfully, they were gone.

Settlers step outside the stockade walls to determine that the Indians and British really left.

15

STARTING THE CHASE

Looking from the behind the stockade walls, we were sure it was another trick. We manned the walls with guns ready and sent out six scouts to check the area. They returned shaking their heads because they couldn't believe what they had found or more to the point, what they hadn't found. They hadn't found a single sign that the redcoats and redskins were still there. Bear and the other dogs were let out of the stockade with me and other folks to handle them. We still found not a single sign that the bloody redcoats and bloody redskins were still there.

We couldn't believe our good fortune. We had all heard tales of folks having to stay inside stockades for weeks at a time during the year of bloody sevens. We had been penned up for only a day and a night. Despite all of our mistakes, we had survived with the loss of all our livestock killed, four settlers killed and a handful of settlers wounded. Of course our cabins and building had been burned but they could be rebuilt. The savages had done their best to destroy our crops but there could be enough saved to last us through the winter. Despite our mistakes, we were lucky.

We were lucky as a settlement but not all people were

lucky. We had four men killed and a handful wounded. To top it all off, Jim Morgan could not find his wife. Jim had hoped that she was hiding outside the fort where the savages could not find her. His only hope now was that she was still alive.

It had been a mistake not to have a well inside the fort. If the savages had decided to strike when the women were out getting water, they could all have been either killed or captured. If all or some had been captured and their lives held hostage for our surrender, we would have to have surrendered. It was a mistake not to have had enough water kept inside the walls to last for two or three days. Water barrels should have been placed to allow us to put out any fires from thrown torches. If the strong winds from the east hadn't blown the flames and embers away from the other buildings, the whole stockade could have burned and we could have all been massacred. If the dry dust hadn't been stirred up by the hoofs of the relief's galloping horses to hide the horses and riders, they could have all been killed. If the bloody redcoats and bloody redskins hadn't emptied their guns firing into the cloud of dust, the militia on foot wouldn't have been able to escape through the corn field. If Bear hadn't roused pa and me, things could have been a sight worse. Almost every survivor prayed a prayer of thanks that sunny August morning at Bryant's Station.

That morning, every bucket, barrel, gourd and kettle was filled with water from the spring. There was enough roasted meat left on roasting sticks where the savages had cooked our stock that they had slaughtered to feed everybody and we all ate. After we ate, the four men who had been killed were given proper Christian burials. The dead savages were rolled down the slope that most of them had had been killed on and covered over with dirt and brush. Nobody prayed over the dead savage redskins.

Just doing the burying and starting cleaning up had us all tuckered out. That evening, we posted guards and arranged for them to be relieved (pa did most of this task) and were glad to get to sleep. We stayed within the stockade walls that night and held a church service Sunday morning.   Then things got as busy as a fiddle at a shucking bee.

We began getting groups of militia from Boone's Station, Lexington, and Harrodsburg as well as other smaller stations. The different leaders then met to decide what to do next.   Men from Bryant's Station had already scouted north on the buffalo trace and came back with word that the redcoats and redskins were on the move and making no effort to hide their trail.

This fact got Colonel Todd all excited. He sure liked the possibility that the redcoats and redskins were on the run and had left such an easy trail for the militia to follow.

The militia force was made up of several small groups from neighboring stations. The different militia leaders from the several different stations kind of cooperated with each other but not always. Daniel Boone headed between forty and fifty of the Fayette County militia and he was under John Todd.   Todd had served under George Rogers Clark on the Vincennes campaign. Another large group of militia was led by Stephen Trigg and Hugh McGary from Lincoln County.

I never did learn much about Trigg. He as from Virginia and appeared to be a man of means. He had connections with a lot of leaders and politicians in Virginia and appeared to have a lot of learning.   John Todd was from Pennsylvania and had a lot of money and learning.   He was one of the men who founded Lexington in 1775. He surveyed, bought and claimed a sight of land. He settled down, more or less, in Lexington and was one of the two men to represent Kentucky County in the Virginia legislature.   He went with George Rogers Clark to the Illinois country and was appointed by Patrick Henry, Virginia's governor, as governor of the Illinois Territory.

Now, we all know a sight about Daniel Boone, him having a book wrote about him and all, and I've no argument with any of the book. Pa and Lige knew Boone in North Carolina where he left just ahead of being lawed for debts. Of course, being lawed for debts could happen to anybody. At any rate, we know a lot about Boone.

Boone had been a longhunter and was as skilled as the best of the longhunters. Lige did say that the Cherokee and Shawnee would watch Boone and steal his catch at the end of the season. That might be so but I got no friends among the heathen to ask.

Hugh McGary is another man entirely. Some have said that Hugh McGary was as crazy as hell. He settled in Harrodsburg, where his family was slaughtered by savages in 1777. Folks claimed that he went crazy after that. Folks claimed that he fed his dogs redskins to make them learn to find them. He was sure hell on redskins after that. Most people in Kentucky didn't blame him. I surely didn't blame him. I got no use for the redskins myself.

McGary's family, like many other people in the colonies, came from Ireland as indentured servants. Like I said before, the indentured servants' comfort or discomfort depended on who their master happened to be. McGary was from North Carolina and like Boone and Lige, was a longhunter. He is supposed to have hunted with Boone but I can't swear to it. Folks that knew him before his losses in 1777 said he was quite tolerable to be around.

This all changed when he discovered his stepson's mutilated remains where savages had left them after they had tortured the boys to death. McGary's stepsons, Will and Jim Ray were out collecting sugar sap at a sugar camp with Tom Shores and Will Coomes. Blackfish and seventy Shawnees heard the sugar making activities and surprised the camp. Will Ray was tortured and mutilated until he was killed. Tom Shores was taken captive and James Ray outran all the Shawnee in making his escape. Will Coomes hid in a tree. James Ray reached Fort Harrod and immediately told his stepfather that the camp had been attacked by the Shawnee. McGary right off went after Jim Harrod and blamed him for not keeping better guards out. He demanded that Harrod send thirty men with him to the sugar camp. Harrod refused to allow that many defenders to leave the fort. McGary pointed his rifle and Harrod pointed his right back at McGary. It looked to everyone there that they might kill each other but Hugh McGary's wife stepped between them and pushed his rifle away from Jim Harrod. Harrod then allowed thirty men to go with McGary to the sugar camp. Folks at Harrodsburg figured it was to make McGary's wife feel better. When the party got to the sugar camp, they found the tortured and mutilated remains of his stepson,

McGary was overcome with rage and grief. When he killed the redskin who happened to be wearing his stepson's shirt, he cut the redskin up and fed him to his dogs.

Since 1777, McGary had been a man looking for a fight. He argued with his new wife and, it was said, slapped her around. He threatened to kill his brother-in-law in view of most of the population of Harrodsburg and was generally regarded as not someone to have dealings with. He was, however, regarded as a good Indian fighter. That's why McGary's suggestions during the officers meeting at Bryant's Station came as such a surprise.

McGary glanced at the wreckage of the 100 acres of corn, the hemp fields and the vegetable gardens where plants had been pulled out by the roots and shook his head. Then he looked at the northeasterly direction where the buffalo trace clearly showed the passage of the hostile force. Turning to face Todd, Trigg and Boone, he said, "I think we should wait for Ben Logan and his men."

During the meeting, anybody who cared to be there could see and hear everything that was said. When McGary suggested that they should wait for Ben Logan to come from Logan's Fort at St. Asaphs, folks were sure surprised. When McGary made his statement, one man I was watching like to swallowed his chew of tobacco. This kind of caution was not expected from Hugh McGary.

"I disagree," Todd was quick to answer. Looking straight at McGary, he said, "This is no time for timidity. We need to strike the trail before they escape."

Now Colonel John Todd was real uppity in the way he answered Hugh McGary. Todd, maybe with thoughts of future elections, said that they needed to get right on the trail before the Indians could escape. Todd might have been thinking that he was only in charge until Ben Logan showed up. Ben Logan outranked him and would take over when he got there. Now when John Todd spoke, there was a sight of people listening. Maybe he felt he had to say what he said because there were so many people there to hear him. I don't know but that is what he said.

Now these men weren't stupid. They knew they would be going up against a force of roughly five hundred hostile savages and bloody British, including the Girty brothers. Looking back, I think most of the men were more scared of being thought scared than they were of the redskin devils. Two mornings before, the women of the fort had walked down to the spring to bring up water. There was no way a man could show fear after the bravery they had shown.

Hugh McGary was insulted by Todd's pointed comments but he didn't kill him, which was surprising to some. The men, less than two hundred, mounted and struck out on the trail. Pa, Lige, and me went with them. Pa commanded that my brothers stay and make sure the women got some protection.

It is possible that Boone did not prefer to serve under Ben Logan. After Boone escaped from the Shawnee and returned to Boonesborough to warn of an attack by the Shawnee, Richard Calloway accused him of being a traitor. A lot of people thought that Boone's in-laws leaned toward the Tory side. I don't know if they did or didn't but like I said before, in Kentucky we had to fight both the red coated British and the redskin savages. Ben Logan had brought charges against Boone. Boone was acquitted of all charges but he didn't think much of Ben Logan after that.

Israel Boone, Daniel's son, was suffering from the fever, sneezing and heavy head that August brings to some folks. You could tell he was in bad shape but he was with the men who left. Aaron Reynolds, the crowing rooster who had shamed Simon Girty the night of the siege, was in the group

.

Pa and Lige scouted the north side of our line of march. Amos and his son Ben scouted the side. The four of them compared information when we camped that night. Our camping spot was the same one used by the devils we were chasing, just the night before. Pa turned to Amos and Ben and asked, "What do you think of what you saw today?"

Ben was slow to answer and I could tell he was choosing his words real careful. "The truth is, I don't think they are trying to get away, I think that if they fight like Indians, that we will whip them but they may know something we don't."

Pa nodded and gestured with his left hand to Lige. Lige shrugged and said, "I was just wondering if it was time for me to get my religion back."

Nobody smiled or made light of his statement. Trees on both sides of the buffalo trace had been fresh blazed by tomahawks. There was no attempt by the redskin devils to hide their trail. Worst of all, there was no sign that any groups had broken away from the main group. None of us figured that the force we were chasing was trying to get away. We all felt like we were being led.

Thinking back on it now, thirty-three years later, we should have figured out what was up. Girty had been trying to get us out of stockades and into ambushes for some time now. He had tried to lure the men of Bryant's Station into chasing a few Indians so they could then be ambushed. He had tried to ambush the relief force from Lexington and Boone's Station. Ambushes was about all that worthless renegade was good for.

My pa had it all figured out.

A settler checks the priming of his flintlock before proceeding.

16

THE BLUE LICKS

I have mentioned Todd, Trigg, Boone and McGary. They were not the only leaders we had with us. Levi Todd, Robert Patterson, Gabriel Madison, John Bulger, John Gordon, Will McBride, Silas Harlin, John Alison, Will Elison, John Beasley, Sam Johnson, Joe Kincaid, Clough Overton, Joe Lindsey and John McMurtry were all part of the force. All were officers but thirty-three years later I can't swear what their ranks were. There may be more that I've forgot.

Aaron Reynolds, the man who had answered Girty at Bryant's Station, was certainly with us. Aaron Reynolds was a rooster of a man given to outrageous swearing when the occasion warranted. He was a brave man.

Boone was very familiar with the Blue Licks. A lick was a place where wild animals came to lick salt. Of course, salt is necessary in preserving meat. The constant attacks by the red dogs during 1777 had prevented the settlers from making salt and prevented salt from coming from east of the mountains. Boone and the settlers figured that the savages would stay north of the Ohio River and close to their fires during the cold winter months. If this had been the case, then going to make salt would have been a good idea. Boone with a party of thirty men left Boonesborough in early January, 1778, for the salt springs at Blue Licks to make salt.

The water from the salt springs was boiled down in large kettles and the salt crystals were scooped off. As sizeable loads of salt were cooked off, the salt was returned to Boonesborough. Boone was a woodsman who would always rather hunt than work. In early February Boone was out hunting for game. He had a good hunt and had his horse loaded down with fresh meat. He was returning to camp in a snowstorm when he ran into over one hundred savages and British Canadians. Boone, finding that escape was impossible, surrendered.

After surrendering, Boone learned that the hostile force aimed to capture Fort Boonesborough. Boone commenced to lie his head off. This was okay because he was only lying to redskins and worthless British Canadians. Boone told them that there was a large number of fighting men at Boonesborough --- so many that they were able to send him and his crew out to get salt. By the time Boone finished talking, they all believed him.

Boone also told them that they didn't have to attack the salt makers, that he would talk them into surrendering. The redskins and the British Canadians must have thought that was a good idea, because that's what they did. Boone went ahead to the salt making party and told them what was going on. He also told them they were outnumbered 4 to 1 and told them that the best chance to live was to surrender.

That is what the 27 men in the salt making party did, they surrendered. There would have been 30 to surrender but three men had just left for Boonesborough with a load of salt. The 27 who surrendered had second thoughts about surrendering in the near future.

Boone said the Shawnee savages kept every promise they made to him. He and the other 27 men were taken to old Chillicothe, on the Little Miami River. Boone always said they were treated as good as savages could treat a person.

Boone acted as though he was right pleased to be with the redskin hellhounds. He told them tales and settled in with them just like he was close kin. The other prisoners didn't take to Boone being so friendly with their captors. The tales some of them brought back to Boonesborough had a lot to do with Richard Calloway accusing Boone of being a traitor.

While a prisoner, Boone gave the impression that he was right where he wanted to be. He went on hunts with his redskin captors and generally fooled them into believing that he was happy where he was at.

Boone was adopted into one of the savage families and acted just like they was blood kin. He acted as happy as a pig in a corn patch. He had shooting matches and hunted with the redskins but was always careful to let some of them outshoot him.

When he saw that the Shawnee were getting ready to march on Boonesborough, Boone waited for his chance and lit out.

After Boone returned and Boonesborough was successfully defended, Richard Calloway charged Boone with treason. None of the settlers or militia at Boonesborough backed up Callaway's charges. Instead of dropping the charges, Calloway went to Logan's Fort and talked Ben Logan into backing up his charges against Boone. The Court Martial was then held at Logan's Fort.

Most folks couldn't see the sense of bringing charges against Boone and he was cleared of all charges. Folks for the most part just figured that Richard Calloway was jealous of Daniel Boone. It was rumored that some of Boone's in-laws were Tory leaning but, as long as they weren't renegades like the Girty's, it didn't matter on the frontier. Add to everything else the fact that Callaway's son, Flanders, was married to Daniel Boone's daughter, Jemima, and you had a real kettle of fish.

Even though Boone was found not guilty, both Richard Callaway and Ben Logan showed that they thought Boone should have been found guilty. The accusations hurt Daniel Boone plenty.

Pa said he figured that Callaway was bad jealous of Daniel Boone. People kind of looked up to Daniel more than they looked up to Callaway. Pa said a lot of folks left the east where they were tadpoles in a large lake and went to Kentucky where they hoped to be a big frog in a small puddle. Now it's only common sense, that when half a dozen tadpoles try to be the big frog in a small puddle, that they will bump into each other.

Boone, by virtue of his experiences in the wilderness and the leadership he had shown during the redskin and redcoat attacks of 1777, drew a lot of respect and admiration. Callaway and others had a problem with that. This jealousy by smaller men hurt Daniel Boone, George Rogers Clark and others.

Richard Callaway was killed by savages on March 8, 1780. Ben Logan was still alive. Ben Logan was leading a force of around three hundred men somewhere on the trail behind them.

When we arrived at the camp where the redskins and redcoats had stopped, Boone examined the camp site left by the savage dogs and their British masters and reported to the rest of the officers that there were at least five hundred of the enemy. The officers met and talked things over. I talked with pa and Lige.

I mostly listened while pa and Lige talked. I may be a slow learner but I had learned a long time ago that I learned more listening to Pa and Lige than I did a talking to them. Pretty soon, Amos and Ben Patton joined us again.

"Well, John, looks like we got them on the run."

"I'm not sure who has got who, Amos." Pa started flipping his knife which was a sure sign he was thinking things over.

"Well, it seems like we got them running."

"We have been following them up the buffalo trace. Their trail is real plain and we aint sent out any scouts or spies to find out what they're doing." Pa flipped his knife again.

"John, what are you saying?"

"I'm saying that everything Girty has done has had a trap or an ambush in it. He baited us with a few redskins to draw us from behind the stockade. He even let the women get water thinking it would show us there were only a few of the heathen. He had a few make a run at the easterly side of the stockade and then had a big group charge at the westerly side. He tried to ambush the relief from Lexington and Boone station. Every damn thing that renegade, Girty, has done has had trap or ambush hid in it somewhere."

Amos turned to Lige and asked, "What do you think?"

Like I said, I learned a sight by listening to my pa and Lige.

"Amos, I think we should have ten or maybe twelve spies out to scout the enemy. We aint got any now. Because we are following such a clear trail on the buffalo trace, we know where they are going." Pa paused and added, "We just don't know what they will do when they get there."

I waited a spell and went over to where Israel Boone was resting. I hunkered down next to him and waited for him to notice me.

"What do you think is going to happen, Israel?"

"What I think will happen is that we will get a little rest and wait for Ben Logan."

"You think so?"

"Maybe hope so is the best way to say it. Pa told Todd and Trigg and some others that we will be facing upward of five hundred ant that he figures we should wait for Ben Logan."

"You think that is what we will do?"

"He also told them that if we attack without Ben Logan, that we should split into two groups and attack from two different sides."

"Do you think that is what we'll do?"

"I think we should wait." Israel Boone paused a moment and asked, "Did you see the two riders Todd sent out?"

"I saw them leave."

"They are going to meet Ben Logan and tell him the redcoats and Indians are waiting above the salt licks and to go straight there instead of following our trail."

I saw that pa and Lige were talking to Boone. I waited until they finished and then joined them. I let pa speak first.

"What did you learn from Israel?"

I told pa and Lige everything Israel Boone had told me. They listened and both nodded.

"I hope that is the way it goes. Aaron, Lige and me are going to spy for a little while. We should be back by dawn. If they leave early, we will catch up with you. Do you understand?"

Of course I told him "Yes pa'" because he was my pa.

"Right now, Aaron, get some sleep."

I spread my wamus and put my pack down for a pillow and went to sleep.

17

AMBUSH AT BLUE LICKS

I didn't sleep near long enough. It was still night when Todd had us roused to travel. I fell in with the rest of them and we made slow going because it was so dark. There was some grumbling, naturally, but not real loud. No one on that march wanted to be the one who exposed us to a night attack by making too much noise.

We stopped our march about three or four miles from the Blue Licks and waited until it began to get light. When dawn was real close, we formed into three columns and made our way to the Licking River and the Blue Licks. We stopped on a high point across from the Blue Licks. From there, we saw some of the savages on a hill across the Licking River. We all saw the savages. Major Hugh McGary led his men across the Licking River. Colonel Steve Trigg followed with his men and finally Major Daniel Boone led us across.

I know that, here lately, folks claim that Todd and Trigg and Boone didn't want to cross the river and wanted to either wait for Ben Logan or follow Boone's plan of dividing the men into two groups and attacking from two different sides. As the tale goes, there was a meeting of all the officers on the river bank at the ford.

These tales claim that Hugh McGary had opposed both these ideas and ran his horse into the Licking River and hollered, "All who aint damned cowards follow me, and I will show you the Indians."

I aint saying the tale is a lie but it sure aint the way I can remember it. I sure don't remember no meeting at the ford and I don't remember McGary running his horse into the River and hollering , "All who aint damned cowards follow me, and I will show you the damn Indians."

To hear folks tell it now, there was fifty or seventy-five men that did their best to tell Hugh McGary that crossing that river was a bad idea. I didn't hear anybody say it. I was some surprised because after talking with Israel Boone, I figured we would be waiting for Ben Logan. We didn't wait.

I do not know what was said or when but I do know that both Pa and Lige expected to report back to Boone a lot further back on the march than where we were right then. I crossed with the rest of the men.

We crossed the river and reformed into the three columns we had been in before we crossed the Licking. Todd and his men took the right side. Trigg and McGary took their men in the middle. Boone and Patterson led us to the left side. We rode up to about two hundred yard from the tree line and dismounted.

Patterson had me and five others hold on to ten horses each. I looped a cord through the bridles so I wouldn't lose any horses if I could help it. I tied the loose end of the cord to my camp ax handle and lodged it the fork of a sapling.

I might have been doing make wok but I was nervous and had to be doing something. I thought it would be easier to be with the men going on the attack.

I remember that Boone was toting a fowler instead of a rifle. I reckoned that his fowler was about as over charged as the Brown Bess I was toting.

Boone and Patterson led their Fayette County Militia toward the tree line. The other columns were moving in the same manner.

I thought about my choice of weapons. Boone carried a long barreled fowler and I carried my Brown Bess. Both were good for short range shooting. Most of the militia carried rifles which took longer to reload but had the advantage of being much more accurate at a greater distance. By closing with the enemy, I wondered what would happen to that advantage.

Boone and Patterson led their Fayette County Militia toward the tree line.

I didn't like being asked to hold the horses. Truth be told, my feeling were a little hurt because I was left holding the horses. Ben was with me and I could tell he felt the same.

"Aaron, didn't we hold our end up at Bryan's Station?"

"We did."

"Then why are we being left behind to nurse these horses?"

"Ben, I figure everybody here has held up their end at least a time or two. Our chance will come."

"I want our chance to happen now."

I don't know why but I was remembering the lad who couldn't wait to go running through the Cumberland Gap. I remembered he had run into a mess of copperheads.

"Steady, Ben, steady."

About that time, Major Harlin led an attack with men still on horseback. Boone and Patterson made some contact and their men began firing. While we watched, Boone and Patterson led their militia with success against the savages. It looked like one good charge might harvest the crop.

Then I checked the horseback charge, expecting to see the same result. I didn't. There were a lot of horses with empty saddles and a lot of militia on the ground. I didn't see Colonel Todd or any of his officers. Most of Todd's Column seemed more interested in finding an escape than attacking the savages and the British.

I'm not trying to slander their courage or their manhood. They were following their leaders, Todd and the other officers, when suddenly there were no leaders left to lead. If they hadn't been out in the open and clear targets, a leader might have rose from the ranks. But they were out in the open and they were clear targets and no leader was able to rise up and take control. Todd's part of the force was outflanked and as soon as one of them had an empty gun, they were attacked by savage devils with tomahawks.

I looked back at Boone's group and saw that he and Patterson still seemed to be making progress. Ben's eyes were locked on his pa who was with Boone.

Looking into the tree line, I saw British soldiers getting ready to fire. I lost sight of what was happening for a minute or two as I worked to control the horses.

Looking into the tree line, I saw British soldiers getting ready to fire.

Ben was yelling encouragements to his pa, the Fayette County Militia and all the Kentuckians in general. I looked up from wrestling the horses to see what had him so worked up but what I saw was the middle column under Hugh McGary beginning to break and retreat.

While I watched, McGary grabbed a horse and rode it to where Boone and his militia were fighting. I couldn't hear what was said but it seemed to me that McGary was warning Boone to retreat.

Todd's part of the force was outflanked and as soon as one of them had an empty gun, they were attacked by savage devils with tomahawks.

Boone gave the order to retreat and his men began a fighting withdrawal. By this time they were outflanked and had to fight through the red devils to get to the Licking River. Some of the other horse holders were leaving and the retreating men were grabbing whatever horse they could. Some were shedding their guns, pouches and powder horns in an effort to escape.

I used my Brown Bess to stop some of the red devils trying to outflank Boone. I pulled a homemade paper cartridge that contained a sizeable powder charge, a .73 caliber round ball and twelve .30 caliber buckshot. I primed the pan from my powder horn and fired again. While I was reloading, Ben yelled. "Pa," and rode one of the horses straight into the fight. All the other horses he was holding ran.

Boone and his men retreated from the battle. I mounted my horse and managed not to lose my musket. I reached down and grabbed the handle of my camp ax and pulled it from the fork of the sapling. This wasn't easy to do because the houses were excited or scared and didn't help me none at all, but somehow I managed.

Now I'll tell you the truth. Every bit of me wanted to get the hell out of there. I didn't want to prove to anyone that I was a brave Indian fighter. I wanted to run, and I might have run but I heard pa saying, "Steady, steady."

Yep, it was pa and Lige. They had finished their scout and had finally caught up with us. They hadn't expected us to move out as early as we had moved.

Seeing pa and Lige beside me calmed me down a right smart. I started to tell pa that we needed to help Ben and his pa but when I turned to point, I couldn't see either of them. Lige yelled something in pa's ear that I couldn't hear because of all the other shouting and shooting. Then pa took my camp ax with the horse cord wrapped around the handle and yelled in my ear, "Follow me."

I followed pa. Pa angled toward a spot between Boone and the river. When we reached Boone, men started grabbing horses. That was when I found that the red devils had already got to the ford and would have been waiting for me if I'd ran that way. I don't know if I heard it or imagined it or if it was pa's voice in my brain but I would swear that over all the noise of battle that I heard pa saying, "Steady, steady."

We could see parts of the fighting that was going on at the riverbank as the retreating militia tried to cross. We later found that some made it and some didn't. The fighting was done with swinging axes and tomahawks, clubbed rifles and muskets, and nerve.

Boone and his men retreated from the battle.

Pa rode up to Boone and asked, "Which way?"

Boone pointed to a spot of the river away from the ford and we all followed his pointed hand. "Cross downstream out of range of those at the ford."

Everyone else moved. Boone pressed the reins of his horse into Israel Boone's hands. I didn't hear what was said but while I watched, Israel was shot. Even I could tell that his wound was a killing wound.

This is another thing I have heard a lot of tales about. I don't know how many people I have heard say as fact that Daniel Boone carried his son out of the battle, across the Licking River, and hid him in a cave where the heathen redskins couldn't find him. He probably wanted to but I am here to tell you that there is no way in hell he could have done it.

There were none of the heathen between us and the spot on the river Boone picked for us but there were plenty behind us that were trying to catch us. Our retreat was a fighting retreat and I had no idea that I could load and fire that Bess as fast as I did. The poor old Brown Bess musket wasn't anywhere near as accurate as a good rifle but it could spread a lot of lead fast. I was glad that pa had me make as many buck and ball paper cartridges as I could carry.

The four of us were the last of Boone's bunch to cross the river. Crossing that river was a chore for a lot of the men. Many of them wore buckskin breeches and the wet buckskin made them slow targets. Men were taking off their breeches and either carrying them across the Licking or were losing them altogether.

Like pa and Lige, I was wearing a breechclout and leggings. I took off my leggings when pa and Lige did. We made it across the Licking and Boone started organizing the men he could still find.

The Battle of Blue Licks gave plenty of opportunity for men to show their bravery and good sense. A good many of the militia took advantage of that opportunity.

Ben Netherland made it across the river at the ford. He stopped to catch his breath and take one last shot at the heathen. He shot and stopped three other retreating militiamen who still had their arms. They fired a volley at the heathen. It wasn't long before Ben had a dozen militiamen giving cover fire to the retreating militiamen trying to ford the river. It's untelling how many more might have died if Ben Netherland hadn't organized the covering fire.

Aaron Reynolds, the rooster who had out-crowed Simon Girty at Bryant's Station, had a horse and was on his way when he saw that Rob Patterson was wounded and down. Aaron Reynolds put him on his own horse and sent him down the trail.

Not all heroics were rewarded. Daniel Boone's nephew, Squire, had been shot in the thigh during the attack. Sam Brannon put him on a horse and mounted behind him. They made for the river ford and crossed safely but Brannon was shot in the back as Squire was able to escape.

I still remember the heroics of Ben Patton charging to help his pa. He was captured and murdered.

Boone and the remaining officers began organizing a defense but, as it turned out, didn't need to. The heathen were more interested in scalping and mutilating the dead and wounded than risking their lives against the living.

Not all of the militia who escaped across the Licking River stopped to give covering fire or to get organized. Some flat out ran like all the devils from hell were after them. Some didn't have weapons and some were wounded.

One of the wounded was Jim Morgan. Jim had left his child with the women at Bryant's station and went with the militia. He had looked along the trail, hoping to find his missing wife alive. Instead, she found him.

She had been the only captive taken during the raid on Bryant's Station. She had loosened the straps that held her when the redskins and red coats were paying attention to setting up the ambush. She managed to escape when the fighting started. She fled across the Licking River and made a wide swing around the fighting. She found her husband, Jim, where he had collapsed from his wounds and exhaustion. She helped him on the trail until we overtook them and put both of them on the same horse. Her escape and reunion was one of the few bright parts of the day.

The heathen red devils, after all the scalping and torturing and mutilating; didn't feel like chasing us after we crossed the river. From where we watched, we could see the savages lining up over twenty captives. I was sure, despite the distance, that I recognized Ben. They seemed to be counting the number of killed on each side. They then pulled out four of the captives. Ben was one of those pulled out. Even with the distance we could hear their screams as they were tortured.

The British were there and did nothing to stop the murdering of prisoners. The whole battle had taken maybe fifteen or twenty minutes. I will never forget that I saw British soldiers from Butler's Rangers attacking us. The British have always been lower than a snake's belly. I will never forget that I thought I saw Jason Smith with Butler's Rangers. I wondered if Ben was chosen to be murdered because he recognized Jason Smith.

That is when I really started hating the redcoats and the redskins. I could understand why Hugh McGary acted like a crazy man. I could understand why he was so filled with hate against the redskins. He felt that way because he was right.

Pa came over to stand by me. I just shook my head and told him, "I know pa, steady, steady."

"Steady aint always the easiest thing to do."

"No pa, it aint."

Lige joined us. He looked tired. It occurred to me that I had never seen Lige look too relaxed. I think I was beginning to understand Lige.

Butler's Rangers attacking.   Photo by Jim Cummings.

I could understand why Lige lived and acted like he did. I hadn't lost a woman that I loved and wanted to marry but I had heard a friend I had known all of my life tortured and murdered.

Pa and Lige led me back to the column.   They didn't say anything and I didn't say anything. There was nothing that we could say.

Boone, McGary and the other surviving officers led us on a barely organized retreat back to Bryant's Station and Lexington. Pa put two wounded men on his horse and Lige would walk for a spell and let someone without a horse ride. I did the same.

We met Logan's force and the officers told him what had happened. Logan moved on to the Blue Licks with some of the retreating militiamen joining him. Pa, Lige, and me went too.

Logan led us on as far as the Licking River. We didn't see any Indians but most of us figured that didn't mean much. Logan returned us to Bryant's Station where he sent for more men. As I recall, Major McGary gathered up over a hundred men. When Ben Logan figured we were strong enough, we set out once again for the Blue Licks.

We arrived back at the battlefield on August 24th. It was almost impossible to tell which corpse had been who. I have heard some folks say that their kin who fell hadn't been all cut up and mutilated but I didn't see any that weren't. Some also said that the wild animals hadn't been at the bodies but that wasn't true either. The pain and anger I felt when I saw what was left of Ben (I think it had been Ben) has never really left me.

We buried all the dead in one grave and did the job as fast as we possibly could. Five days in the hot August sun hadn't done the bodies any favors. I still hate the British. I still hate the Indians.

EPILOGUE

Well there you have it. If I aint taught you nothing else, I hope that I've taught you that you can't trust Indians.   That and that the British aint worth a damn either.   I don't reckon that if I lived another fifty years that I'd trust either of them.   I stayed in Kentucky. I was in on several more expeditions against the savages. I was there when General Wayne whipped them at Fallen Timbers, chased them right to the bloody British fort and rode in front of the fort, just daring them to shoot.

The British did not gain a foot of ground from their ambush at the Blue Licks.   The whole fight was just to act out their general wickedness. Some blamed the leaders for the defeat at Blue Licks. History has blamed Hugh McGary. The defeat at Blue Licks caused George Rogers Clark to lead another military expedition against the Ohio Indians. He destroyed Chillicothe and five other Indian towns and either took or destroyed all of their food supplies. Clark showed the red devils that we could be as destructive as they were and that they could be as vulnerable as we were.

I was with Clark on his expedition against the Ohio Indian villages. While we were there, our spies brought in a white man who claimed he had just escaped from the Shawnee.   He was getting treated real good as any person who escaped from the Shawnee would be treated.   Right away, I recognized him and stepped up.

"I was hoping to see you again, Jason."

"You said his name is Jason?" The militiaman who asked seemed a little puzzled.

"What name did he give you?"

"He said his name is John Steele."

"He is a damned liar. Back in North Carolina, he was a damned Tory named Jason Smith. I saw him with the renegades at Bryant's Station. I saw him with the British at the Blue Licks."

"Are you sure?"

"Yes I'm sure, and something else, my friend Ben and his pa were both captured at the Blue Licks. They both knew this man for a lying Tory in North Carolina. I have wondered if that was why they were tortured and murdered after they were captured."

"Then I think this is a man Clark and Bowman will want to ask some questions."

"Probably. If he gets back to the settlements, some others will want to talk to him."

I turned and walked away. Jason was no longer being treated like a man who had been a prisoner of the Shawnee. He was being treated like a captured renegade prisoner. I knew that he would never get back to the settlements alive. I didn't give a damn.

I stayed in Kentucky. Built up a nice farm and a large family. I'm forty-nine years old now and satisfied with life in Kentucky. Every day since that morning of August 19, 1782 has been a gift that I hope I have appreciated enough.

Like many other old pioneers, I fought in this last war with the hell-spawned British. William Whitley died as he lived, taking to the field against the cursed savages.   He died in Canada fighting Tecumseh's bunch.

I was at N' Orleans with Andy Jackson. It was a privilege to shoot at so many redcoats.

A great many of the old pioneers have either moved on from Kentucky, like Daniel Boone, or have died. Many others or are no longer with us. Boone and most of his extended family migrated to the Spanish lands in Missouri.

George Rogers Clark has been ruined by the government he fought for. They claimed they did not get receipts of all the bills Clark signed for when he was taking the northwest and protecting the Kentucky settlements. I think they are lying sons of bitches. He can't make a dollar now without being sued for it. He lives in a cabin on his brother's land and drinks to forget the way his country misused him.

Some, like Lige have settled down and live peaceful lives. Maybe I will too. My wife, Lucy, keeps telling me that I need to calm down and be thankful for what I have. She said this last bit of fighting, all the way from Canada to N' Orleans had better be enough for me. I've still got no use for the redcoats or the redskins.

ABOUT THE AUTHOR

The author, Charles E. Hayes, MSgt, USAF (Ret.) spent 24 years in the United States Air Force. He is a former school teacher and an avid re-enactor. He currently helps other veterans through the auspices of the Disabled American Veterans in Kentucky.

Made in the USA
Columbia, SC
24 July 2023

20801101R00083